THE
BEAST
OF
LOUGHBY ISLAND

THE BEAST OF LOUGHBY ISLAND

MATT DOYLE

ISBN: 979-8-88785-028-3 (Paperback)

Library of Congress Control Number: 2023950748

Any references to historical events, real people, or real places are used fictitiously. Names, characters, and places are products of the author's imagination.

Book design by Allison Chernutan.
Edited by Carol Kudeviz, Patterson Hood, and Miriam Tepper.

Printed in the United States of America.

First printing edition 2023.

emily@fracturedmirrorpublishing.com
Fractured Mirror Publishing
Knoxville, Tennessee

www.fracturedmirrorpublishing.com

Have you ever wished there was a book dedicated to you?
Well, you can make that dream a reality. If this story tickles
you in all the right places, then you are exactly who it was
written for. That being the case, you are welcome to take this
as a dedication to you. Providing you understand that you
aren't the only one, of course.

But first, a warning. If you are indeed considering
writing your name below, you need to be aware of
a few things with this story:

Violence stalks these pages, draped in a veil of blood.

The themes contained herein may offend some.

You probably shouldn't get too attached to the characters.
If they have a name, they're fair game.

If that's fine with you, then I have good news!

This book is dedicated to:

____

[Enter name above]

*"And much of Madness, and more of Sin,
And Horror the soul of the plot."*

- Edgar Allen Poe, The Conqueror Worm

Foreward

Less than ten pages into *The Beast of Loughby Island*, there is a werewolf attack so viscerally descriptive, that it is next to impossible to not imagine the grotesque aftermath Doyle so expertly devoted to the page. The Lycanthrope subgenre of horror is one of such potential, that it allows its writer to touch on various topics, all seen through the metaphorical lens of becoming the beastly version of yourself in ways that alter who we are.

Loughby Island is going to be a divisive one to say the least, but aren't the best horror tales ones that don't cater to what a reader expects from it? Stories that dare challenge their reader and invite them to experience dread and horror in ways that can't simply just be passing experiences. These stories tend to be the ones which nestle firmly under our skin, living there rent-free and never quite leave.

Doyle's knack for giving his viewers characters you care about, horror that feels real and stories which never feel like they're re-treading familiar ground, speaks on how much of a unique voice the writer has. It would be a great disservice not to inform you readers that not only are you about to read a book that will last, but are about to read a story from a writer who I will gladly go on record saying, will be one that we all will be talking about for years to come.

I will most definitely be revisiting *The Beast of Loughby Island* and I am quite excited to be among those who champion Doyle and this special story.

Jerry Smith
(Writer/REUNION, Composer/PUPPET MASTER: DOKTOR DEATH)

CHAPTER ONE

JOE ATKINS HATED SAILING AT NIGHT. HE'D WON THE BOAT on an episode of *Bullseye* in the late 80s, and while it still worked, he'd learned years ago that he knew nothing about maintaining speedboats. Or sailing them, for that matter. As a result, his little *delivery* jaunts were choppy affairs. Even so, he had faith in the machine. It had been built in the Midlands, meaning it was like him: solid, British, and unrelenting.

That didn't stop him from struggling to see, though. This sort of mission required a degree of stealth, so he couldn't exactly light up the way ahead. Tonight, the sun had seemed to set early, too, meaning he couldn't rely on the low light to alert him when to slow down near the island.

But this was necessary work. Kent needed to be cleaned up, and if no other fucker was going to do it, Joe damn well would. Best of all, this time, both his kids were coming along for the ride. That was enough to make him smile, at least.

A grunt came from the back of the boat, and Joe hissed, "Oi! Keep him quiet! We're just coming up on the bank."

"You heard him," Robbie chuckled, and the unmistakable sound of a hand slapping the back of someone's head cut the grumbling short.

Joe swung the boat to the right and brought the speed down as he angled towards the muddy bank. It was the same place he always parked up when dropping off an undesirable, and he preferred to stop side-on so he didn't have to get his feet wet.

The boat drifted onto Loughby Island with a satisfying *bump*, and Joe turned toward his son. "Help your sister. And you," he growled, grabbing his cargo by the shoulder and shoving him towards the land, "Ger'off."

"Which way?" Laura asked.

Joe nodded his head toward the woods at the top of the hill. "Stick close. You don't wanna get lost here. You'll end up indoctrinated, or whatever."

"I can't see," the man said, his voice muffled by the sack over his head.

Joe shoved him in the back, forcing him forward. "Shame that, ain't it? Keep quiet, walk where I say, and *maybe* I'll let you know if you're gonna walk into anything."

The man's shoulders sagged, but he started walking. Though tempting to let him just walk into trees, Joe was true to his word. If nothing else, he didn't want the idiot drawing unnecessary attention if he made a racket. To that end, he kept his own voice low as he explained to his kids, "This little Hellhole has turned too many people soft. Still, it keeps the bleeding hearts all in one place, don't it?"

"I can think of a few more I'd like to send here," Robbie said. "That bloody Carl Rogers down the street for one."

"You and me both, lad." Joe hauled the man to the side, avoiding a large rock, and asked, "And *why* can't we just chuck him over here?"

"Because the police, blah, blah, blah," Robbie replied, his eye roll creeping into his voice.

"You better take that seriously, you little prick. You try to do one of these deportation trips with a local fella, and we all get in the shit. Lost little lamb like this one," he said, slapping the man on the shoulder, "they'll never know."

"They knew about Dougie Walters," Laura sighed.

Joe grimaced. That had been a misjudgment on his part, one that almost got all of them in trouble. "Only because he's tecÚically still local, even if he is a worthless waste of space."

Robbie shrugged. "Didn't he used to be a teacher or something, though?"

Joe fought to keep his body language strong and upright. "What you *were* don't mean shit, lad. Only what you *are*. Take me. I was a foreman. Ran that factory like a well-oiled machine in the best and the worst of times. Now look at me. I worked every day of my adult life until they closed that place. I paid enough in taxes to fund a small town of dole scroungers. I *earned* my break. Earned the right to let someone else look after me for a change. Yet you look at how those people look at me. At us. Like we're fucking scum."

"But one of these tossers wanders in," Laura growled, giving the man a kick up the arse, "they get all the help in the world."

"Exactly. That's why I do this. Why I want you two to, as well. We're keeping the streets clean. Keeping people out of *our* benefit pool. Some other place wants to fund their lifestyle, let 'em do it, but I won't see our town fall under the rule of dossers and immigrants. Even if none of them in town know what we're doing for 'em, *we* do. Working in the shadows, fighting the good fight."

"Like a family of superheroes." Robbie stood taller then, his pride almost moving his steps into a march.

"Proper British vigilantes," Laura added.

"*That's* what we are," Joe smiled and led the group farther into the woods. Even without a torch, he knew the route well enough now that he wasn't about to get them lost. It was the one thing he liked about this place: It never changed. The people of Loughby Island never wanted to develop more land than they had to, and the population never swelled. It just trickled upward then subsided again if one of Joe's drop-offs didn't stick around.

Up ahead, torchlight shone through the darkness, and a voice drifted between the trees.

"Get down," Joe hissed, dragging the man to the floor and gripping his coat tight. He crawled quickly to the side, pulling the man with him. "This way. Get behind the bush. Keep quiet, all of you, or I fucking swear, what I do is gonna be far worse than anything that cop does."

The group huddled together, and Joe heard one of his kids inhale sharply as the voice drew near.

"You'll never guess what happened to me today."

It was a woman. Joe relaxed a little. If it came down to it, he was pretty sure he could take any woman in a fight. Certainly far easier than he could that turncoat Cole, anyway.

The woman laughed as she came to a stop a few feet from the bush. The torchlight swung around a few times, barely catching the tips of the leaves as she said, "That's right, fuck all."

She lingered for a moment, then walked on, her voice slowly fading into the night. Well, that's the sleepover shift for you. How are you two? Not missing me too much, I hope?"

They waited in silence for a moment, then Robbie asked, "Dad…what if she finds the boat?"

Joe shook his head. "She won't. I picked that spot 'cause you can't see it from the hill. The patrol here doesn't go down the bank unless they spot something."

"But what if she does?"

"Look, I never said this wasn't dangerous. Think about the bigger picture, lad. Now, come on. Let's get this done."

They continued on in silence until they reached the edge of the woods. There, Joe grabbed the man by the shoulder again, pulling him to a stop, and removed the sack from his head.

The man took a deep breath and asked, "Where are we?"

Joe pointed down a little stony path. "You follow that, you'll find the town." He put one hand behind his back and signalled to his kids. "They're well-known for taking in waifs and strays, so you shouldn't have any trouble fitting in with the other misfits."

"But…I can barely see. Can't I at least have a torch or something?"

"You won't need one. Someone'll find you soon enough." Joe felt the dampness of the rag Laura had placed in his hand and, for the second time that night, he reached around the man and forced it against his face. The struggle was minimal this time, like the guy was resigned to his fate. After a moment, he dropped to the ground.

Robbie looked down at the man. "So, what now? Should we take his bag? Or his wallet?"

"We'll have none of that," Joe said, his tone firm.

"Yeah, we're the good guys, remember?" Laura scoffed. "Heroes don't steal."

"Exactly. Plus, we get caught with his stuff, that ties us back to him, don't it? Why do you think I said we don't use our names here? We have to be careful to not let him, or anyone else who might hear us, know who we are." Joe cracked his neck, and, for a moment, he thought he saw something in the darkness ahead. Like two eyes peering over the hill. He frowned. "Let's get back to the boat. Keep quiet, right? Just in case that cop doubles back."

The family headed back through the woods. Joe could feel the excitement pouring off the kids. Even moving silently, there was no hiding it. They kept giving each other playful glances and their bodies were full of the same nervous tension they had when he took them to their first football games. In a way, he felt like he was betraying them right now. This was exactly how he wanted them to feel joining him at his work. He should be over the moon at that reaction, but he couldn't even bring himself to join in with the smiles. Joe wanted to believe the excitement they all felt explained their faster pace but knew that wasn't it. He was leading the way and moving quicker than he would normally. With speed came the increased risk of noise, and with noise came the chance they'd be caught. This was reckless.

But something was *off* about those eyes. Joe couldn't place it, but something told him they were *wrong*. Worse, he was certain he'd seen them again. *Yes,* he told himself, letting his eyes glance quickly to the left. *Whatever it is, it's flanking us.*

"Probably just one of those foxes I dropped off," Joe muttered.

"You say something?" Robbie asked.

Joe waved his hand dismissively and stepped out onto the muddy bank. Giving the area a quick glance, he didn't find any sign of either the cop or the weird eyes. *Still*, he thought. *Better to play it safe.*

"Okay," Joe said, turning towards his kids. "I'm gonna make sure the coast is clear. You two wait here…and…"

Joe's mouth dropped open. A dark shape rose behind his daughter. It was a man, but not a man. Now, unable to look away, Joe realised what was wrong with those eyes. It was hard to tell in the dark, but where there should have been white, the eyes looked black. But the irises-those shone like a dog's, except in a bright crimson.

It all happened too quickly.

Laura screamed in pain as the monster effortlessly tossed her to the side.

Robbie turned towards his sister's voice. "What the fuck?"

The creature dove onto Robbie, its rage-filled screech turning to a gargle of blood as it sunk its teeth into his throat. The moment they hit the sand, it whipped back its head, ripping away a chunk of flesh, spraying blood as it snapped its jaws, and swallowing the raw meat.

A single tear fell from Robbie's eye, and something clicked in Joe's head. "You bastard," he roared and ran towards the beast. He hit it hard with his shoulder, forcing it away from his son as they both tumbled to the side.

Joe was not the young man he once was. Back in his youth, he'd get in brawls regularly, especially after football, and he could take damn near anybody in a fight. These days, he was slower, and he had a few extra pounds of flab on him, but he was still tough. And right now, he needed to be.

He knew Robbie was done for, and he struggled to fight back the tears for that. But he couldn't see Laura. His daughter had enough sense to run. Whether she went to the boat or the cops, it didn't matter. He had to keep her safe. Buy her time. So, he rose to his feet, his chest puffed up and hands out ready to box.

The creature rolled up onto all fours, and Joe advanced, raining punches into its face and screaming with rage with each swing. He threw everything he had behind each blow, seemingly keeping the monster from rising to its feet.

Left, right, left, right, right, left.

Each punch found its mark, drawing a grunt or a snarl from the beast, its anger rising with every impact.

When his arms began to sag, Joe changed tact and smashed a hard boot up under the monster's chin, causing it to yelp in surprise. He stumbled back, panting loudly as he growled, "Have…that…you fuck!"

The creature turned one eye towards Joe, pulled its lips back into a malicious smile and rose to its full height, giving it an extra foot or two of terror to catch the glow of the moon. Everything about it screamed *wrong*. Its cruel expression, bloody gums, and dripping fangs were somehow neither wholly man nor beast. Yet the familiar, but disparate parts were still enough to make the thing look somewhere between canine and human, all wrapped up in a big, bloody bow of nightmares.

Joe's blows hadn't done a damn thing. The monster was waiting for him to punch himself out. Or maybe it was just testing him to see what he had. And now it stalked toward him. Joe became hyper aware of every little thing it did. The way it idly flexed its clawed hands. The visible breath that billowed out from its throat with each, long step. The rise and fall of its chest as it lowered its head and cocked it to the side, studying him. Its human-like shape made every movement a mini horror of its own, and the speed at which it approached was terrifying.

Before he could react, claws pierced Joe's cheek. Teeth buried themselves in his stomach. The beast shoved him back by the head, its hand ripping through his lower face, the pain mingling with the discomfort of the cold, wet ground slamming against his back.

Lying on the muddy bank of Loughby Island, Joe realised he could no longer move. He had grown cold. Numb. He was vaguely aware of the sensation of his insides being dragged outside, each tug accompanied by a happy grunt from his attacker. Joe knew he'd been too slow to save Robbie, but right now, he was at least distracting the thing long enough for Laura to get farther away.

Mustering what little resolve he had left, Joe blinked and forced himself to look upward. *If I'm gonna die,* he thought, *at least I'm gonna do it looking at Britain's beautiful, starry sky.*

The monster seemingly grew tired of the taste of Joe's guts and slowly crawled forward until its face hovered over the man, blood and saliva dripping onto what remained of his cheek. Joe couldn't help but stare now. A human-like head, distorted by a short, menacing snout. Oversized teeth that stopped it from fully bringing its lips together. Whatever this thing was, it looked like it wasn't always what it had become. The way it twitched; it was like it was in pain.

Joe didn't have the time to let his clarity turn into sympathy. Mouth stretched wide, the creature snapped its head forward, digging its teeth into Joe's face. He felt his eyes pulled from the sockets, and just for a moment, he saw the back of the monster's throat. Then, there was only darkness.

Chapter Two

TOM DANIELS FELT A HAND ON HIS SHOULDER. THE DARKNESS moved around him in quick jerks. Next, the sounds of the world began returning.

"…Alright?"

Tom opened his eyes. He blinked and rolled over, pushing up into a sitting position. The woods loomed behind him, and he ached all over. His head was spinning and letting everything come back into focus in the dim light of the half moon was painful. It took a moment to notice the man squatting down next to him. He had dark, unkempt hair that hung halfway down his neck, and a thick, neatly trimmed beard. He also looked very concerned.

"You alright?" the man asked again.

Tom frowned. "I think so. Where are the other three?"

The man tilted his head to the side and raised an eyebrow. "Other three?"

"The three that brought me here. They were talking about being heroes or something."

The man sighed. "Lad, do you know where *here* is?"

"Not exactly."

"Okay. Come on, I'll fill you in." He stood up and offered a hand.

Tom stared at the man for a moment. He'd had enough of strangers approaching him tonight, but this one seemed more genuine in his friendliness, at least. And, at this point, things couldn't get much worse. So, he took the hand that was offered and allowed himself to be pulled to his feet. Once he'd regained his balance, he reached down and picked up his bag. It didn't feel any lighter, which he was willing to take as a small win.

"The name's Selwyn Bonner. You?"

"Tom. Tom Daniels. You don't sound like the other three. You sound…Irish?"

Selwyn chuckled and started walking. "Irish? Do I, now? Well, there's a reason for that. Don't worry though, you haven't ended up that far away. You're still in Kent, tecÚically. This is Loughby Island. You ever hear of it?"

"No," Tom replied, pulling his parka tight. He looked around and realised that he'd obviously been led pretty far inland by his kidnappers. The coastline wasn't visible, and where he was right now, it was mostly open grasslands guarded by aged, waist-high stone walls. Further ahead, the silhouettes of buildings were slowly coming into view. "It's a little place off the coast," Selwyn said, leading Tom to a wooden gate and onto a stony path that cut through an open field. Up ahead, lights shone through the darkness. "Now, you mentioned three people. Did one of them happen to bang on about immigrants stealing his benefits?"

"Something like that. " He thought back, trying to pick out exactly what he'd heard from beneath the haze of the night's events. "And dossers. He said dossers were just as bad."

"Ah, Joe's varying it up then. I'm guessing the other two were a boy and a girl, probably a bit younger sounding." Selwyn looked over his shoulder at Tom, and when he received a nod in response, continued, "You've encountered the Atkins family. Proper Little Englanders. Or just plain bastards, as I prefer to call them."

Tom stopped, his face hardening and body tensing. "I'm

sorry, but…where are we going? It's just…after tonight, I'm not exactly keen on just following some stranger through a field in the middle of nowhere."

Selwyn nodded, and stopped to look at Tom. "That's fair. Well, look. You're not the first person they've done this to. And even without the Atkins lot, we still end up with a couple of people just sort of finding their way here by accident. So, we take care of the hospitality."

Panic beginning to build, Tom took a step back. Selwyn held his hands up in response. "Calm down, lad, I don't mean it in some sort of gangster movie sort of way. What I'm doing is taking you to the pub. I'll get you a drink, food if you need it, and we'll see if we can talk to Robert Cole. He's the guy in charge of the local police."

Tom groaned. "The police and I don't really get along."

"I'd guess not. If Joe dropped you here, then you probably weren't moving into the area or anything. Rob's not gonna hurt you though. Like I said, you aren't the first to be dumped here. You've not done anything wrong."

Tom thought about it for a moment. He wasn't entirely sold on the idea of heading to the police, but there was something very honest about Selwyn. If nothing else, he really believed this was the best way to help. That was important. Most people Tom encountered just wanted to move him on, not help. For that reason, he decided to go with it. "Okay. Thank you."

They continued the journey down a steep slope, and Tom found himself grateful there hadn't been any rain. The stony path was nice. Unlike the rough ground they'd stared on, it was built from gently rounded cobblestones and looked like something out of an old British sitcom.

"You're right," Tom said, trying to make out the size of the town they were approaching. "I was just passing through Kent. Figured I'd find somewhere to lay down for the night and get going again in the morning. Some guy asked if I was okay. He sounded friendly-ish, but before I could get a good look at him…well, next thing I knew, someone put a rag on my face, and I woke up on…a boat, I guess?"

"I thought you may be travelling, given the bag. That's why I wanted to help you. You ever see *Rambo*?"

It took Tom a moment to register what Selwyn had asked. He frowned. "Rambo?"

"Yeah. The film. The first one, mind. *First Blood Part One*."

"No."

"Really? Sylvester Stallone? You've never seen it?" Tom shook his head. "Ah, it's great! See, there's this drifter, JoÚ Rambo, right? He wanders into this town and the Sheriff is all nice to begin with, but he's really thinking, 'we can't have a vagrant like this dirtying the place up.' So, he tries to force the fella to leave. It all gets really messy, and there's this big hunt through the woods. Rambo does some real damage. Loughby Island is a nice little place. I figured we wouldn't want something like that happening here."

"So, you're helping me so I don't flip out and attack someone due to a lack of hospitality?" Tom replied, incredulously.

Selwyn laughed. "No, I was joking with you. Not about the film being great; you're missing out. I doubt you're a danger to anyone, though. I mean, look at you there with your Britrock special and all that."

Tom let out an involuntary chuckle, pulling the forest green parka tight. "It's a warm coat."

"I bet it is." Selwyn gave Tom a pat on the back and pointed to a group of buildings placed haphazardly at the foot of a small hill. He led Tom down the bank and onto an open street. "This is Loughby Town. Or part of it, anyway. There are a few other places scattered around, but we group them all into one town. No sense naming more than one on such a small island, right? It gets a bit neater the farther in you go. Or the streets run mostly straight, anyway. The Kestrel's Crown is down here and to the right."

"The Kestrel's Crown? How'd it get called that? Most of the

pubs I passed back on the mainland were the something-or-other's arms."

"Well, see, it was supposed to be something more mundane. I think it was The Merchant's Boots or something like that. The guy they hired to do the sign though got a bit drunk and painted this great big bloody kestrel instead. The thing's sat on a throne with a red robe with white fur trimming and everything. And, it has a crown that's hanging around its neck. Pat, the pub landlord, asked the guy why it has a crown around his neck, and do you know what he said?"

Tom shrugged.

"He said, 'It's a kestrel, innit. Its head's too small to wear the thing.' Well, Pat loved the whole concept and just kept it. So, it is now and forever more, The Kestrel's Crown."

"That's another joke, isn't it?" Tom asked. "Like the Rambo thing."

"Actually, no. That one's true. Sometimes, the crazy bollocks isn't bollocks at all."

The pair rounded a corner and, to Tom's surprise, the sign hanging above the door at the pub was exactly as Selwyn had described it. The kestrel would have looked regal had it been in a children's book, but it was just plain ridiculous in this setting. The rest of the building had an old worldly feel to it though—all white paint around big windows with greying roof tiles.

Inside, the mood was more akin to a fictional local pub than the often-portrayed pit of misery he'd seen on his travels. People filled the space, laughing and chatting. Near the back wall, a guy was butchering something on a karaoke machine to the point that he might as well be making weird noises into the microphone. A small gathering pelted him with peanuts. The singer didn't seem to mind, though, trying to catch the flying nuts in his mouth as he warbled.

Selwyn, noting Tom's poorly disguised amazement, asked, "You not been in a pub before?"

"Not like this. The older ones I've been in were full of old men that sounded like—what did you call him—Joe? The more modern ones were full of people on the pull. None of them were this cheery."

"Hey! Big Sal!" The voice cut through the chatter with ease but disturbed no one. A man waved to Selwyn, the drink in his hand nearly sloshing onto his slicked back, dirty blond hair.

Selwyn smiled and led Tom towards the man. "Tom, this is Superintendent Robert G. Cole. And the sod knows my name's Selwyn, but he was too drunk to get it right when we first met."

"And I've made a point of not getting it right since," Robert said, straightening his tie. "So, Tom, was it? This time of night, I'm guessing you didn't come here on a tourist trip."

Tom kept his eyes down, trying not to say too much. "Yeah, Tom. And no, not exactly."

Selwyn gave Tom a pat on the shoulder. "It's fine, you can trust him Tom. You good with sausages? Of course you are, you look like you'd like sausages. Pat! Get Tom here some sausages and something to warm him. I'm paying. *I'll* have my usual." Selwyn turned back towards Robert and added, "Another Atkins drop. Had his kids with him this time by the sounds of it."

"For fuck's sake. Think you'd be able to identify them?"

Tom shook his head. "They snuck up behind me and knocked me out with something on a rag. When I woke up, they'd put a bag over my head. I might be able to recognise their voices, though."

Robert rubbed his chin. "Do you think you'd be up for giving a statement? Not right now, obviously, but maybe in the morning?"

"I mean, sure, but I don't really have anywhere to stay. Or money to pay for somewhere."

Robert nodded. " I'd offer you a cell, but I can't imagine that's your first choice."

"Don't worry about that," Selwyn said. "You can stay at mine, or Pat could probably put you up for the night. Pat! You'd take in an Atkins drop, right?"

A man with thick-rimmed glasses and a permanent scowl stepped up behind the bar. "Whiskey for Selwyn, and coffee for the other fella. Milk's off, so it's black. Sausage, mash, and gravy on the way. And unless he can clean dishes, there's no room at the inn."

"Thank you," Tom said and looked to Selwyn. "If it's not too much trouble, I'm okay to stay with you. Honestly, I could do with a shower. If that's okay?"

Selwyn smiled. "Sure thing, lad."

"This happens a lot," Robert said. "You'll usually find a person or two happy to help out. They're good people here. Oh, speaking of guests, you haven't seen Dougie, have you?"

Selwyn nodded. "Sure, he's in his castle. Or he was this afternoon. Said he was working on something that might get his life back on track."

"Hmm. Well, Jenny took a call from the mainland. They reckon he stole a shovel. Oh, and he took a photocopy from a book at the library without paying."

"And they felt the need to call that in? Was the shovel diamond encrusted or something?"

"End of line discount in a bargain store."

Tom scratched his head nervously. "Should you really be talking about all this in the open? Isn't it confidential?"

"In this case, not really," Robert said. "We all look out for Dougie around here. A lot of us knew him on the mainland, and he was very well liked. Plus, I'm having trouble taking this too seriously."

"Not a big reader?" Tom tried. "Or not a gardener?"

Robert shook his head. "Gardener, yes. Reader, not really. When you spend a chunk of your day reading reports written by some of my team, you lose your love of the written word. That said, I think they said this was a map he'd photocopied, anyway, so it probably isn't heavy reading."

Selwyn let out a bemused chuckle. "What did he want a map for?"

"Who knows? It was from that book that caused all the tourism last year. Uh, *Darkness Dwells Here*. You heard of that one, Tom?" Tom shook his head and Robert continued, "It's a study of the island. It used to be home to a bunch of feuding religious types, all with their own favourite demons. The short version is they all wiped each other out and the island was left uninhabited for a long while."

Selwyn sighed. "Then, someone noticed the book existed, posted about it online, and all of a sudden we were overrun by sightseers with a love of the morbid."

"They left pretty quickly when they realized the religious stuff had all disappeared a long time ago." Robert shrugged. "Just tell Dougie to keep out of trouble if you see him, yeah?"

"And you tell him to stay out of here too," Pat added as he shuffled past. "He's still barred after that incident with the darts."

"Incident with the darts?" Tom asked.

Robert started to respond, but was cut off when his radio crackled and a voice squeaked, "Sir?"

Robert sighed. "This is Cole. It's Friday night, Larry. If you've got yourself stuck in the station again, you can wait until Jenny finishes her patrol."

"No, sir. It's…fuck…"

There was a moment of silence, then another voice came through, female this time. "I've got this, it's fine. Rob, you really need to get down here. We've got a big problem."

"Which is?"

"Are you still in the Kestrel?"

"Yeah."

"Then you need to get outside, and I'll explain while you walk."

Robert frowned and stood up. "Fine. I'm on my way." He turned to Tom and said, "Come by the station tomorrow morning. Selwyn will show you where we are."

"Is everything okay?" Tom asked.

"Can't see why it wouldn't be," Robert replied, picking his

jacket up from the bar stool and pulling it on. He gave a short wave to both Tom and Selwyn, downed the dregs of his beer, and walked out.

Pat wandered back over and dropped a plate in front of Tom. It was mostly a pile of mashed potatoes with a couple of sausages chucked across the top, and the whole thing swam in a thin gravy. It was more than Tom had eaten in a few days though, so he tucked in eagerly. He swallowed an oversized mouthful, burning his throat, and asked, "What do you think that was about?"

Selwyn downed his drink, waved to Pat, and pointed at the empty glass. "Probably nothing. Constable Larry Flanaghan is afraid of his own shadow. He's also the clumsiest cop you'll ever meet. Nice fella, but you wouldn't leave him in charge of your house." Selwyn shrugged. "Larry probably broke something. Wouldn't be a first-time offense. Either that or he spooked himself and now they tecÚically *have* to investigate it."

"Ah," Tom mumbled through another mouthful.

"You'll learn that quick enough. Bar people like yourself turning up unannounced, nothing really happens around here. That's part of why we all love the place."

CHAPTER THREE

SUPERINTENDENT COLE PULLED THE VEHICLE UP ONTO THE mud and parked. He *knew* Inspector Gill couldn't be right; things like that didn't happen on Loughby Island. Even so, he took the van. Deep down, he also knew that Jenny wouldn't make something like this up.

Farther along the water's edge, the speedboat lay banked on the island. No mistaking whose it was. He'd been in the audience when Joe won the thing. They may not have seen eye-to-eye in recent—or not so recent—years, but they'd been friends once. Close even. For that reason, he hoped Joe wasn't mixed up in this.

Larry sat on the hill near the scene, his arms wrapped tight around his knees, looking pale. Robert stopped next to the young Constable. "Are you okay?"

"I will be. Thank you, sir."

Robert nodded and walked on, heading up the hill to where Inspector Jennifer Gill had squat down. "So, let's see this—"

Robert's words caught in his throat when he saw the mess. Chunks of flesh dotted the ground—*literal chunks*—and an intestine hung dripping from a tree branch at the edge of the woods. As Robert shone his torch across the remains, the familiar face of Robbie Atkins stared back at him. The other corpse didn't have enough face left to be sure, but really, who else could it be.

Jenny said, "I bagged the wallet for that one. It's Joe Atkins."

"Shit." Robert let the word draw out, unable to pull his eyes away from the single eyeball hanging out of the pulp that substituted for Joe's face. The mainlander was a lot of things, most of them nasty, but he didn't deserve this. "Any idea what happened here?"

"Hell," Jenny replied. "Hell happened here."

"I can see that."

"Without looking at the remains under some proper light, I won't be able to say for sure. Did you bring the body bags?"

Robert nodded, still unable to break his inadvertent staring contest with Joe's body. "How are you okay with this?"

"I'm not. But Larry is worse. How about you?"

Robert rubbed his chin. "I am most definitely *not* okay. We may have another problem, too."

Jenny stopped bagging a torn piece of clothing and looked up. "Oh?"

"They were doing one of their drop-offs. The guy they left here, Tom, mentioned kids, plural. Which means Laura is potentially somewhere around here too."

"You don't think this Tom did this, do you?"

"He didn't seem the type. His clothes were clean, too. Or clean of blood anyway."

"Maybe he did it then changed."

Robert nodded. "Yeah, I know. But without evidence, I can't do anything about it. Which means I'm gonna have to speak to Selwyn. He's the one taking the guy in for the night."

Jenny stood and brushed her ponytail over her shoulder. "At least Selwyn won't spread what's happened around the town. It may be worth you dropping by his place though, at least once we get all this back to the station."

"Yeah. But, I'm gonna need to make some calls first. The

mainland may have seen someone come out this way. Do you think Larry's able to do a search for Laura?"

Jenny wrinkled her nose. "Honestly? I think getting away from *here* will do him some good. Providing she's not here because she *got* away, of course."

"Okay. I'll go have a word with him, then grab the body bags." Robert walked back down the hill, uncomfortably aware that he was struggling to keep the bile in his throat down.

CHAPTER FOUR

MAGGIE BAKER HAD BEEN PART OF LOUGHBY ISLAND AS LONG
as anyone. Her grandmother claimed that her family had history
with the island, before the current attempts to populate it.
Old stories aside though, the island suited her. There weren't
many cars around, so instead of engines revving, the sounds of
people talking occasionally serenaded the streets. Literally just
talking; no arguments, no slanging matches, just happy chats
about the day. You wouldn't think it to look at her in passing.
Maggie had clung stubbornly to her teenage mohawk, albeit a
far shorter version now that her hair had begun to thin, and she
had maintained her youthful spunk and playful attitude—but
her brand of noise was not aggressive unless it was warranted.

"When it comes to music, it is abso-fucking-lutely warranted,"
she chuckled to herself, turning up the speakers and launching into
a jovial sing-along with a punky explosion of anti-Governmental
sentiment. She half-bounced, half-shuffled around behind the
counter, loving every moment of the throwback to her concert
days.

The sound of the bell above the door crept in above the
guitars, and Maggie looked up to see who had entered. She gave
a nod in greeting.

"Evening, Maggie," Selwyn said. "I tell ya, you should bring this stuff to the Kestrel. It'd be nice to hear someone half-decent on the karaoke."

"Not a bloody chance," Maggie replied, smiling. "The difference between that lot and me is I *know* I can't sing. Besides, who'd be here to serve you late-night shoppers if I did that? Now, who's this?"

The newcomer shrugged. "An easy target, apparently."

"Ah, you're a drop-off. And what was your crime? Did you tell the bugger off for giving you shit?"

"No, I was just passing through."

"Ah, and he thought he'd pass you somewhere else." Maggie sighed. "Joe doesn't like…many people, actually. Used to be a right shit when I ran a store on the mainland. He did nothing but complain about how I was ruining a 'good, British shop' with my American noise. His daughter was worse, though. Mouthy, racist little thief. I banned her in the end.

"To this day, I suspect my twins ran off to do their own things because of Laura's abuse. She did rather resent getting her milk from, what did she call them? Bloody foreigners. Even worse, bloody foreigners born in the area. Anyway, it left me to pick between saying sod off to retirement or closing the family business. As you can see, I took the noble option."

"That's because you're a national treasure," Selwyn said, grabbing a basket and heading for the selection of coffees stacked precariously at the end of the aisle. "You want to watch this one, Tom. She could say whatever she wanted, and nobody around here would dare bat an eye. I reckon she'd get away with murder, you know."

Maggie smirked. "Right now, I'm nice enough not to try. Let's make sure we keep it that way, eh?"

"I wouldn't dream of pushing your buttons, Maggie, you know that. You got any more bacon in?"

"Delivery's tomorrow." Maggie turned to Tom and asked, "So, your name's Tom, is it?"

"That's right. Tom Daniels."

"Good. If it had been Henry, we'd have had issues."

Tom narrowed his eyes. "Cheating husband?"

Maggie clapped once and pointed a triumphant finger at him. "Close enough. Husband that walked out when the kids got—what was the phrase he used? Too needy. Or 'born,' to you and me. He was a prick anyway. Still, it does leave a sour taste in my mouth when I hear his name. I only kept his surname because I couldn't be bothered with the paperwork to change back to Akinyemi. That and to remind me not to make the same mistake again. And that is a method that has worked for a good few years now, I can tell you."

Tom crossed his arms and shot Maggie a cheeky grin. "Now, tarring all Henrys with the same brush is a bit Joe Atkins, isn't it?"

Somewhere in the snack aisle, Selwyn laughed.

"I like this one, Selwyn," Maggie said. "For that, I'll give you a free go at the contest. Correctly guess what tattoo I have hidden away on my body, and you win a prize."

Maggie crossed her arms and waited. Tom's face had scrunched up, and he was looking around the shop, clearly hunting for clues. He wouldn't find any, though. That was the beauty of the game. Most people ended up thinking it was music related and had some deep meaning about rebellion. In truth, it was a badly drawn weasel she'd had put on her hip on a whim in her early twenties. She never had it changed or covered up because she didn't believe in having regrets.

Finally, Tom seemed to settle on his answer and said, "A flaming skull?"

Maggie pulled her glasses to the edge of her nose and looked down at him, a serious expression on her face, but a smile fought to break through. "And what is in the skull's mouth?"

"A knife. With a serrated edge, like you see in war films."

Maggie stared at Tom, then slapped the counter and smiled. "Nope. No skulls on me. I am many things, but a cliché is not one of them. Try again whenever you want, though. It'll cost you a pound."

"What do I win if I get it right?"

"I'll let you see it," she replied and gave a cheeky wink.

"The mystery of Maggie Baker isn't just what she got drawn, but where," Selwyn said, dropping a basket of items onto the counter.

"And no fucker has come close to the 'what' yet," she added. "Consequently, none of them have seen the 'where,' either."

"With such a generous prize on offer, I'm surprised people aren't queuing up around the island to have a go," Selwyn replied.

"I can't help it if my beauty is so intimidating," Maggie said, flicking her curled, scraggly grey hair. "Now, what have you got here? Puerto Rican coffee?"

"A peace offering for Dougie," Selwyn said. "We had a minor blow up the other night about electricity use."

"Oh, yeah," Tom cut in. "That other guy mentioned him in the pub. One of the ones who, well, left me here, was talking about him too. Who is he?"

"Old Dougie Walters is an infrequent visitor," Maggie said. "Used to do lectures on theology and dead languages in one of the local universities but made some bad decisions and lost everything."

"Bad decisions? Like stealing?"

"Gambling," Selwyn replied. "Mostly. The vandalism probably didn't help either, from what I heard. The local council don't take kindly to graffiti, especially when it's on their windows."

"No, what Dougie did was activism, not vandalism." Maggie replied, firmly. "There *is* a difference."

"In intent, sure," Tom shrugged. "It's still tecÚically against the law though, right?"

Maggie smiled sadly. "Strictly speaking, yes. But when the right cause finds you, or the right experience shakes you up enough, you don't care. Sometimes, what others would view as criminal ceases to be a hypothetical last resort and becomes the only realistic option you have left. You'll also find that the ones most strongly opposed to what you're doing are often part of the problem. Nobody shouts louder about a riot, for example, than the people who caused it. Vilification is a powerful weapon, especially when wielded by those who set the scene. As for Dougie, he was too naïve to notice that those who were too invested in quashing the rights of those he fought for were pulling the strings when he started to fall. I still believe that."

Selwyn chuckled. "One to remember there, Tom. Maggie likes a good conspiracy theory."

Maggie rolled her eyes. "And Selwyn likes to ignore evidence. You look at the when, where, and who, and Dougie didn't just fall in with a bad crowd. He fell in with a very specific crowd with very specific links. They nudged him progressively deeper down his own rabbit hole until two things happened. First, he started eating his own tail by verbally attacking his closest colleagues for all sorts of minor, past mistakes that they'd already learned from. Second, he was acting irrationally enough that he lost all credibility in the eyes of the law."

"Or, he could have just made bad decisions," Tom tried.

Maggie shrugged. "Oh, he certainly did that. No matter who tries to manipulate you or force your hand, the choice is always yours to make. That's a lesson worth remembering."

"That thing tonight sounds like bollocks to me, either way," Selwyn added. "Why Dougie would steal a shovel and a photocopy of a map."

"I'm sorry, what?" Maggie repeated the words slowly, making them a question. "That does not sound like Dougie."

Selwyn shook his head. "That's what I thought too. Still, it's not like he held up a bank or anything. I'll speak to him if he's home."

"He had plenty of trouble with Joe and his lot too," Maggie said, nodding to Tom. "Largely on account of him being very loudly progressive and very justly disparaging of their views.

When it finally reached a point that they could add 'and homeless' to his list of *crimes,* his fate was sealed. They used him as an example of what happens when you stop being bigoted. Get woke, go broke, and all that nonsense."

Tom grimaced. "Ah. And his castle?"

"A shed a little ways behind my place," Selwyn replied. "We can't get him set up with a proper house, because even if someone built one, he'd need to pay council tax, and he's in no position to do that yet. He won't accept any sofa surfing offers, so a couple of us built a shed for him. Well, it's more of a small summer house, really. It's not ideal, but it gives him his own space, for the most part. He piggy-backs off my electric, hence the argument. I never knew him before his fall from grace, but I'm told he was a nice guy."

"He still is," Maggie said. "I knew him because he had enough patience to teach one of my little terrors. It made me sad to see him become so erratic when it all came crashing down. Still, if he's back on the coffee, that means he's got something going on. Maybe he's starting to clean himself up."

"I hope so. If he's home," Selwyn said, glancing back to Tom, "I'll introduce you to him. You can share war stories." He counted out some notes and handed them over the counter. "Here you go, Maggie. Pleasure doing business with you."

Maggie handed a five-pound note back. "Take the coffee for free and put my name on it too. He came in pissed out of his head quite recently; I'm guessing that was probably the same night you two argued. He was yelling about some sort of darts problem. I refused to sell him any more alcohol. He wasn't best pleased. So, coffee seems like a suitable peace offering from me too."

A scream echoed from outside, loud enough to cut through the music. Maggie hit pause on the CD player. Everyone stared out the front window and saw nothing. No further cry came.

After a moment, Maggie said, "Huh. This place is normally far more quiet."

Selwyn laughed. "It was until this little tearaway got here. See that, Tom? You've even set the foxes off. We better get you back to mine before you start affecting the house alarms too."

Chapter Five

LARRY'S HEART POUNDED.

He thought he'd seen Laura Atkins hiding behind a bush, but when he got close, she took off. He couldn't blame her, really. He wanted to do the same thing when he saw the crime scene. Knowing that it was her brother and father, too…the Atkins family wasn't popular in Loughby, but he wouldn't wish that on anyone.

The woods on the island were difficult enough to navigate in the daylight. At night, they were worse. And when you were trying to find your way through them while following someone running in a blind panic, they were impossible.

Snap.

Larry spun around, aiming his torch into the darkness.

Nothing but trees. Again.

Larry turned and continued forward. *Someone* was following him. He'd noticed the sounds shortly after losing Laura. They were too loud to be made by one of the island's indigenous foxes, which meant it had to be human. At first, he thought it might be Laura herself, but there was no way she'd managed to double back behind him without him noticing.

Plus, this person is far calmer than she is, he thought, struggling to avoid breaking into a run.

Larry tightened his grip on the torch and pushed onward. The trees must end eventually. And that meant either his pursuer would stop following him, or they'd have to come out of the shadows, and Larry would know who he was dealing with.

And I'll know where I am then, which means I can radio this in.

Up ahead, a small, flickering light pierced through the gap between the trees, bringing relief wrapped in a dim glow. Emboldened now, Larry allowed himself to quicken his pace.

Snap.

This time, Larry didn't turn. He just kept going until he stepped out into a clearing. A few feet away, was a shed. The light inside was intermittently flashing.

That meant it had been left on for a while. Larry had installed the thing himself, and when it first happened, he'd figured out that the only way to stop it was to turn it off, count to five, and turn it on again. He had no idea why the light did that, but Dougie was always getting at him to look at it again. In truth, he had tried everything he could think of to fix the thing. He did know that Old Dougie Walters was aware of the temporary fix, though, which means he either left in a hurry, or he was…

"Fuck," Larry muttered under his breath.

Larry glanced over his shoulder and scanned the woods. Still no sign of his pursuer. Satisfied he wasn't about to be jumped from behind, he moved towards the shed, slowly, preparing himself for another sight like the one out by the bank. As he crept around the side of the building, several large holes and a downed shovel came into view. The flickering light from the open door showed marks in the ground next to one of the pits, like something had been dragged out of it, then lifted.

Larry steeled himself and stepped around the corner.

There was no sign of Dougie outside.

Just inside the open door, blood stained the floor. Larry closed his eyes, took a deep breath, opened them again, and stepped inside.

The shed had been set up with a sofa bed, a desk, and a single multi-socket extension cable running from Selwyn's place. Normally, Dougie kept it clean and ordered. This wasn't as messy as Larry expected, but it *was* out of the ordinary. The kettle was upturned with the last remnants of water pooling in its body. A small pile of books had been scattered in a corner on the floor, and the sofa bed had been pulled away from the wall. There was no body, though the blood stains on the floor and walls were a strong enough indication that something bad had definitely happened.

The desk was cluttered, too. Papers were scattered all over it and a muddy, steel box sat on the floor by its leg. Larry moved closer, being careful not to disturb anything. There was a map that looked like it had been photocopied from an old book. The illustrated landmass was adorned in lines that weaved and crossed at odd points like a caffeine-fuelled spiderweb, and the words at the top of the page read 'The True Ley Lines.' There was no mistaking that it depicted Loughby Island. The Southern bank, the dip where the town had been built, and the woods were all very clearly marked, as was the little lake in the North-eastern corner.

Laid next to the map was a piece of acetate with indiscriminate shapes marked with terms like 'town' and 'dock.' There were a couple of symbols scattered across the sheet too, though they weren't anything Larry recognised as normal map markings. It looked like it probably fit on top of the torn page but had been moved during whatever had happened. Next to all of this sat an open book. It was dirty, and the yellowy-brown pages now featured faded words and images.

There was a stack of cleaner paper containing handwritten copies of the rune-like text from the book. Under each line were notes and what he assumed were translations. In the margins were a scribbled set of numbers that looked like map coordinates and some sentences with a few phrases circled.

Lupine Pestilence. I am judgment for any son of man that has wronged you. Feast on anger. A beast for beasts. Spread the purge by tooth and claw.

Larry glanced back to the old book and studied the illustration on the right-hand page. The monster at the top of the page had an unnaturally elongated face. It was clearly canine, though not the head of any dog you'd see in England. Or anywhere else for that matter. For one, actual dogs didn't have long straggly hair hanging down to their shoulders.

The creature's body was hunched up but vaguely human. It was bony and had strands of hair and flesh hanging off it. Stretching out behind the monster was a set of torn, hole-covered wings. They expanded towards the edges of the page and looked like they'd been drawn as ragged curtains cut to shape rather than things you could actually fly with. Its tail, hairless and rat-like, snaked around clawed, humanoid feet, equally as bony as the rest of the thing's body. It sat on what looked like a simply drawn altar and was posed to reach one, unnaturally long and bony hand out towards the bottom of the page.

Here, three figures were drawn. The first was a man reading from a book. The second appeared to be the same man, though he was on his knees, and his nails had grown in length. The third picture was of the man covered in fur, with a canine-like face and legs and long, sharp nails. It was hunched over awkwardly, flashing its fangs seemingly in defiance of its strange movement.

Larry shivered.

Snap.

The sound came outside the shed this time.

Larry gritted his teeth. He didn't know if what he was looking at had anything to do with the mess with the Atkins family or even what had or had not happened to Dougie.

A quiet scratching drifted through the silence, and Larry glanced down to see the extension cable twitching.

Then, the shed was plunged into darkness.

Larry grabbed his extendable baton and whipped it out to

full length. He held it out and used his free hand to unclip his PAVA spray, just for good measure.

The scraping of nails against the wood caught his attention at the back wall. The sound moved around the side of the shed and started slowly moving towards the door.

With the possibility of his life being in danger, something clicked inside Larry. He'd spent most of career being afraid. One of his first call outs had turned violent, and he got a real kicking from a thug growing pot on his roof. Ever since then, he'd been jumpy. He wasn't sure why he stuck with the force, outside of not wanting to have to admit to his parents that he was too scared to continue. They'd been so proud of him, after all. That was why he took the job on the island. It was quiet.

This felt worse than that rooftop encounter, though, and to his surprise, Larry's body told him to act, not run.

He stepped through the door and pivoted towards the sound, unleashing the PAVA spray without hesitation. Something in the dark scream-roared in pain. Larry froze. The creature was close enough for him to catch sight of thin, dark fur splaying out haphazardly from its hands as it pulled them up to guard its face. Its palms were bumped with scars and ridges that made them look almost canine.

Before he could fully realise what he was looking at, the partially blinded monster lashed out a hand against Larry's arm, slamming it into the shed, and all but severing it part way down the forearm. What was left hung limply at a right angle, his finger locked in place, still discharging the spray, and causing it to mix with the blood that pumped from everywhere the flesh was no longer connected.

Larry screamed and fell to his knees. He scrambled against the mud, almost falling into one of the holes. Below him, lay a slab of partially uncovered stone. The half moon gave just enough light for him to pick out one of the symbols from the altar in the old book.

Warm breath ran over the back of Larry's neck. His head turned to face it, but he saw only teeth. The force of the monster's jaws as it bundled him into the hole was overwhelming, like it could snuff out any resistance he had as easily as blowing out a candle.

Larry faded, thankful for the small mercy that was the impact of his skull against the old, buried concrete, thrusting him into darkness.

Chapter Six

SELWYN POINTED UP A LITTLE HILL AND SAID, "ALMOST THERE now. My place is just up here."

Tom nodded. He was beginning to show signs of tiring. It wasn't the easiest walk on the island, and Selwyn was sure Tom hadn't had the easiest night of his life either.

"It's not the biggest place in the town," Selwyn continued, trying to keep the silence from hanging around too long. "Being this far out has its advantages though."

A little way in from the hill sat a solitary cottage. Much like the Kestrel's Crown, it had a vintage feel to it, but there were tell-tale signs of modern convenience. The UPVC door was undoubtedly new, and the satellite dish on the roof was certainly not Victorian. The windows seemed too clean to maintain the retro touch and lacked the natural dusty coat of the ones at the pub. There was also a slightly opened drain with a crowbar next to it.

"Welcome to my humble abode," Selwyn said, taking his keys from his pocket. "Like I said, it isn't—"

A loud, animalistic scream cut off Selwyn's words, somewhere towards the rear of the property. Tom frowned and asked, "What was that?"

Moments later, another scream followed.

"Sounds like the foxes are having a bad evening." Selwyn pushed his keys into the lock, gave them a turn, and pushed the door open, leading Tom inside. "That's the biggest disadvantage to living in this house, in particular. See, the foxes don't make too much noise in the town. Up here, though, closer to the woods, they think they own the place."

Tom hung his parka next to Selwyn's on the coat stand. He placed his bag against the wall and asked, "What's the biggest advantage?"

"The other people don't make as much noise up here. They're like anti-foxes like that." Selwyn spread his arms out to the room and added, "So, this is the living room. As you can see, the kitchen over there is open plan. Upstairs, you'll find two bedrooms and the bathroom. I remember you saying you wanted a shower, so head up whenever you want. The smaller room is the guest room, by the way. I'm guessing you have more than one set of clothes in that big old bag of yours, but if you need to wash any, let me know, and I'll chuck them in the machine."

"Thanks," Tom said, taking in the room. The first thing that sprung out at him was the large bookcase filled with hardback books with familiar titles. He nodded at them and said, "I didn't know any of the comic publishers released hardback collections."

"One or two. Most of those are custom, though."

"When you say custom…" Tom said, sliding a book off the shelf and carefully opening the pages.

"Ah, well, I collect the individual issues, then I commission an artist to do some custom cover art for me. There's a fella over on Wilkes Street that puts it all together like the one you're looking at there. Only charges a couple of drinks at the Kestrel. Mostly because he likes the superhero stuff too and this gives him a chance to read them without paying for them."

Tom placed the book back, pulled another collection from the shelf, and looked at the cover. "How old are you, Selwyn?"

"Now, that's just rude. If you must know, I'm forty-three.

And before you start casting aspersions on your hotel manager for the evening, let me tell you, being middle-aged and relatively comfortable financially is exactly why I *can* indulge in this stuff. It's not a reason for me not to."

"That's fair." Tom placed the set back on the shelf and walked over to the mantlepiece that sat above a decorative fireplace. He looked at the single photo sat in the middle, showing Selwyn standing outside the property with another man of a similar age. "Your brother?"

Selwyn lowered himself onto the comfy looking sofa and smiled. "Husband, actually."

"Not home right now?"

"Not unless you know how to summon the spirits of the dearly departed, no."

"Oh. Sorry. That's worse, isn't it? Losing a partner, I mean. Worse than a brother."

Selwyn laughed. "You don't have to panic so much. Yes, though. If you knew my brother, it's definitely worse."

"I was an only child," Tom said, sitting himself into an armchair to the side of Selwyn. "A couple of people I knew had brothers, though, and they were always arseholes."

"Ah, see, mine wasn't entirely bad. The problem was my parents kinda favoured him. That went to his head a bit. Now, my Nan, she favoured me. I think that was in response to the whole Billy-being-treated-better thing. So, when she died, she left everything to me."

"Including this place?" Tom guessed.

"No, it turned out Granny Bonner squirrelled her money away, and nobody knew about it. There was enough for me to get on the property ladder a few times over, though, so that's what I did. I moved over here from Drogheda and made a couple of strategic purchases. Now, I get a modest income from rental properties."

"So, why live here? It sounds like you could live pretty much anywhere."

"Ah, now that was this fella Frank's fault. See, the original owner passed away with no family. The Government put it up for auction to clear his debts, and we both took a fancy to it. Frank, he was a stubborn bastard, so he just kept outbidding me. Until he hit a point that he bid more than he actually had.

"We both saw the potential in the place, though, so we cut a deal. We split the cost, and decided to do the place up ourselves, with the intent to share the rental income. Well, to save on travel, we both stayed here, and, before we knew it, we realised we wanted to make that a bit more permanent. Together."

"You mean…?"

"That's right. Frank was my husband."

Tom rubbed his chin and asked, slowly, "You don't have to answer this if you don't want to, but what happened?"

"To Frank, you mean? About two years ago, he was out checking on another of our joint ventures when he got rear-ended. The lady had a record of being drunk behind the wheel as long as your arm, or so I'm told. Frank died on impact. She got a few days in the hospital, and a few months in prison."

"Oh."

Selwyn forced a smile. "I said the same thing when Robert told me what happened." Selwyn sighed, patted his legs, and stood up. "Anyway. I'm gonna get the kettle on. Why don't you have that shower. I insist on that. You smell like you've been lying down on a muddy hill or something."

Selwyn walked to the kitchen and half-filled the kettle. Once it had boiled, he grabbed a teabag, chucked it in a mug, and set about drowning it. Seeing it was well and truly at one with the water, he took a teaspoon and started stirring, trying to match the sound of Tom's steps on the creaky stairs.

Selwyn heard the door to the bathroom shut—a sound that followed both bedroom doors opening and closing—and made his way to the bookshelf, pulling the collection that Tom had been looking at. He walked over to the sitting area by the bay window at the back of the room, nudged the window open, and sat down, placing the mug on the windowsill. Selwyn let his hand drop down outside the window, allowing his fingers to brush the flowers he'd planted as a memorial.

"The kid's got taste. Or accidental luck. This set right here was a great story, Frank. I know, I know, you never saw the point of my collection. You were more about the classic novels, and all that. But I've managed another week without killing these flowers. So, if I can get out of my comfort zone and take care of one of your favourite things, you can grin and bear one of mine, too, can't you?"

Selwyn opened the cover, taking in the first issue in the set. "See, this one's set a little way after the one we read last week. What's happening is—"

A movement in the darkness behind the house drew Selwyn's attention. A shape sat staring at him. Selwyn stared back, narrowing his eyes as he tried to focus. The ears were distinctive but familiar enough for him to get an idea of what he was looking at. "Big ol' fox, that one. The light's catching its eyes strange, too. Still, you know the rules, Frank. We feed them, and they don't bother us, right? The everlasting pact between man and beast. I'll be right back."

Selwyn went back to the kitchen and opened the fridge. He pulled out a tray of scraps that he'd put aside for just such a visitor. The sound of the boiler clicking off came as he shut the fridge, so he made a quick detour to the bottom of the stairs and yelled, "Tom, the guest bedroom's up on the left. You'll know it when you see it; it's the tidy one. I'm gonna head out back and feed a fox. I'll be back in a minute. Help yourself to a drink if you're down before I'm done."

"Okay, thanks," Tom's voice came in response.

Satisfied, Selwyn went back to the kitchen, opened the back door, and stepped out of the house. He made his way around to the bay window and was unsurprised to find that the fox was nowhere to be seen. They always scarpered when he brought the food out and always came back by the time he was back inside.

Smiling, Selwyn walked out to where he'd seen the fox and set the tray on the grass. When he turned to walk back to the house, he found the fox sitting right there in his path next to the wall. Selwyn jumped slightly, then laughed, expecting the animal to move at the sound. When it didn't, he shook his head and said, "You're a brave one, aren't you? Your food's over here."

The fox still didn't move.

"Well, I've got to get going, so if you'll excuse me."

Selwyn took two steps forward.

The fox still didn't move.

Something inside Selwyn screamed that this was wrong. It wasn't a fox. Its hair sparsely covered greying, human-like flesh lit by the bay window. The unhealthily raggedy body wasn't built to stay on all-fours. Ears, recognisably pointy, sat on the side of its head and far too low down to be vulpine. Thick black claws, longer than they should be, flexed at the tips of human-like hands. "What the hell are you?" he whispered, his eyes flicking to the side to check the distance to his front door.

Selwyn took one slow step backwards.

The monster charged, clearing the distance between them before Selwyn could react. It barrelled into him, knocking him to the ground. Selwyn tried to roll with it, forcing clawed hands away from his chest and sides as he did so, but this wasn't like any other fight. This thing stood like a man, looked like an animal, and moved like something in between. It scrambled against him wildly, not jockeying for position like a human but rather trying to simply catch him.

And catch him it did. Selwyn was on his back with the monster's weight against his body. It lunged forward, bringing its face towards his. Selwyn reacted on instinct, forcing his hands into the creature's mouth, holding its teeth apart.

Time slowed, then. Every drop of spit spraying from the beast's thrashing tongue glinted. Its rancid breath billowed from the back of its throat. And, for just a moment, as his strength began to fail, the thing's teeth grazed his head.

A loud *crack* of a crowbar forced the monster away from Selwyn, sending his arm along for the ride. Selwyn rolled over and onto his knees, clutching his broken hand as he cried out.

"Shit! I'm sorry!" Tom yelled. "I was only trying to hit…what was that?"

"I don't know," Selwyn whimpered.

To his side, a dark shape loped away into the shadows, snarling and yowling in frustration.

Selwyn swallowed his pain. "We need to go. Now."

Tom dropped the crowbar. He helped Selwyn to his feet, and they both started running towards the town, away from the creature. "Where?"

"The police station. Robert's gonna want to catch that thing before it kills someone."

CHAPTER SEVEN

ROBERT COLE COULDN'T BELIEVE HIS EYES. HE'D ONLY COME out to the front of the station because the newbie on the main desk said he had a visitor. He honestly hadn't expected to see Laura Atkins sitting in the waiting area. Given the condition her family was in, he'd feared the worst. Yet here she was, albeit looking somewhat worse for the wear.

When she saw him, Laura stood up and said, "You've got to fucking help me."

The slumped body language and torn, bloody clothes were enough to worry Robert, especially given the state of Laura's father and brother. "Come with me," he said and held the door to the main part of the building open.

Laura nodded and walked past him. "You have weapons, right?" she asked. "Guns?"

Robert looked at her. She wasn't just asking, she was pleading. He frowned. "We do, but we only use them in very specific circumstances. We've *never* needed to use them in Loughby."

"Is a monster a specific enough circumstance?"

Robert stopped. "Laura, what do you mean a monster?"

Laura hadn't turned around, but the tears were clear in her voice.

"They're dead. My dad and my brother. They were killed by that…that *thing*."

"Laura, why were the three of you on the island?"

Laura shrugged, still keeping her back to him. "Social visit."

Robert kept his voice measured. Low, calm, but forceful. "The truth, Laura. It's important."

"We were delivering an undesirable."

"I've met him. Did he kill Joe and Robbie?"

Laura shook her head. "I told you," she whispered. "It was a monster."

"Okay. We can talk about that. Laura, listen. Do you feel up to…" Robert paused and rubbed his chin. "We need someone to identify the bodies."

Laura immediately tensed up but said nothing.

"We don't have to do it, yet. I'll tell you what, you come down here, and we'll find a quiet room. I'll get you a coffee, and we can talk about this monster. How does that sound?"

Laura nodded and Robert led the way to an interview room, guiding Laura to a chair. "Wait here. I'll be right back."

He walked down to the coffee machine a few feet from the door and selected a milky coffee with two sugars. The machine clicked and gurgled, meaning it was working and not jamming up like it had been for most of the morning. Robert grabbed his radio. "Larry, it's Robert. You may as well come back. Laura Atkins is here."

The machine finished pouring its cheap, caffeinated water. Robert grabbed a black coffee for himself and returned to the interview room. Laura was looking at least twice her twenty years. Her eyes were red and tired, and she looked frail. Not at all like the little hell-raiser he'd had to drag out of Maggie Baker's shop when she was twelve.

Robert pushed the first cup towards her and sat down, pressing the button on the small audio recorder on the table. "Milky, two sugars. You still drink it like that, right?"

Laura nodded.

"Listen, I'll be honest with you here. The guy you dropped off tonight? He likely *will* press charges, and I'm going to have to deal with it. So, what you say here is going to affect that. Given what's happened, though, I would like you to be as open as possible. Can you do that for me?"

"Yes."

"Okay. Take me through what happened when you arrived on the island."

"Me, Dad, and Robbie had a guy we found in town. We walked him through the woods at the top of the hill where we docked."

"Was he able to see where you were taking him?"

"No. We had him, uh, *bagged*, Dad called it. We had a sack on his head."

"Did anyone see you?"

"I don't think so. We had to hide, though. One of the…one of you guys was patrolling, I think. A woman. She said something about a sleepover shift?"

"I know who that was," Robert replied. "When she left, presumably without seeing you, what happened?"

"We took the guy to the hill outside the town and took the sack off. Dad told him he'd be fine here, and we knocked him out."

"Knocked him out?"

"Chloroform."

"Jesus Christ, Laura."

"We didn't want him to call for help while we were still on the island."

Robert sighed. "Okay. So, what then?"

"We left him at the top of the hill and headed for the boat. When we got to the bank, Dad seemed pretty spooked. He started to say something about checking if it was safe for us to get back on the boat and…and…" Laura started to sob.

"Take your time," Robert said. "I've seen…I know this can't be easy."

"Something grabbed me," Laura said, throwing force into her voice, like she was trying to *make* herself talk. "It threw me aside, and I landed near one of the trees. Robbie turned around and it tore his throat out. I couldn't move, I just lay there in the dark. Dad tried to stop it, but…but he couldn't. It had already killed Robbie, and it was like Dad couldn't even hurt it. I made myself get up, and…I ran. I saw that Dad was dead, and I ran. While it ate him, I ran away."

"Running away was probably the smartest thing you could have done. Can you describe this person that attacked you?"

"It wasn't a person," Laura snapped. "I already told you. It was a monster."

"This monster, then. Can you describe it?"

Laura paused and looked Robert in the eyes. When she spoke, her voice was quiet. "You wouldn't believe me if I did."

"Try me." When Laura didn't respond, Robert added, "Please, Laura. It's important."

"It looked like a fucking werewolf," she whispered.

"A werewolf?"

Laura shook her head. "See? I told you. I saw it. I watched it kill my dad and my brother. And it started tracking me when I was trying to find my way back to the town."

"So, to be clear, you mean a literal half man, half wolf. Walking upright like a human, but with a wolf head, fur, and glowing yellow eyes? That sort of thing?"

"No. Its eyes were mostly black. The irises were red. It had hair, but there wasn't much of it."

"Let's assume you saw exactly that. Laura, you must know that werewolves don't exist. I can believe that you saw what you said, but this wasn't a mythical creature. It had to be a guy in a costume. Some nutter that wandered over here, probably for the same sort of reasons as you—"

Laura slammed a fist on the table, cutting him off. "No! A human couldn't do what that thing did."

"Of course they could. People do some terrible, terrible

things, Laura. And yes, to a point, the ones that do *are* monsters. But at the core, they're still people."

"Take me to the bodies," Laura hissed.

"I'm sorry?"

"I said, take me to the bodies."

Robert shook his head. "Fine." He pressed stop on the recorder and led Laura down the hallway by the coffee machine. At the end, he gave the door a knock and pushed it open.

Inspector Jennifer Gill stood at the back of the room, studying a set of photos. She looked up and frowned.

Robert waved his hand and said, "Laura here has come to identify the bodies. I'm assuming they haven't been picked up while we've been talking?"

"No, and are you sure about that?"

"Do it," Laura said.

Jenny looked to Robert, and he gave a nod. She sighed and slowly unzipped the body bags.

Laura stepped closer and burst into tears.

"Can you confirm the identity of the two bodies?" Robert asked.

"It's Robbie and Dad."

"Okay. That'll do. Jenny, can you zip them back up, please?"

Jenny reached out to pull the first zip, but Laura stopped her with a stern, "Wait." She pointed to the wound on Robbie's throat. "It did that with its teeth." She moved her finger to the deep cuts under his shredded shirt. "Those were claws."

"What is she talking about?" Jenny asked.

"Laura says her brother and father were killed by a werewolf."

Jenny raised an eyebrow to Robert, and he shot her a look that said, 'let it play out.'

Laura moved to the other bag. "The face was its teeth, so was the stomach. It used its hands to pull…pull things out." She turned away and wiped her eyes, staring at Robert. "Examine the bodies. You'll see. There will be teeth marks and shit like that. Those aren't human injuries."

"Laura. You've had a rough night."

"Neither are these," Laura cut in, pulling part of her damaged sleeve aside to reveal a set of cuts on her arm.

Jenny stepped forward and looked at the wounds. "You need to see a doctor."

"Not right now, I don't. Not while that thing is out there."

"Laura, there's no such thing as werewolves," Robert reiterated.

"Why won't you believe me?" Laura screamed. She pointed at her father's corpse and added, "Did he really mean that little to you? You were friends. He told me that. Don't you want to catch the monster who did this to him?"

"He named your brother after me, Laura. I may not have seen eye to eye with Joe for a long time, but we grew up together, and yes, that means something. That's why I won't entertain this crap about mythical monsters. I will catch *the man* who did this."

Laura looked at Robert and laughed, the sound cracking. When she spoke, her voice was desperate. "You know what? You never cared about us. If you did, you wouldn't have arrested my dad. You wouldn't have hauled Robbie out of school for telling people the truth about those scroungers crossing the channel. You wouldn't have taken a job with these island losers, and you'd believe me right now."

"Laura, that's unfair. Your father assaulted a man. Your brother tried to instigate an assault against a classmate based on his parent's nationality. And I took the job here because I *wanted* it. And you? You aren't a saint, but I do know you're the most honest of the three of you. But a werewolf? You're in shock, Laura."

Laura shook her head. "This was a mistake. Of course it was. I forgot, didn't I? I've seen the news. I've been on social media. I've seen what the police are like. You were never gonna help an ordinary person like me, because you lot are the fucking bad guys."

"Far too many of us deserve that title," Jenny said. "But right now, in this moment, we're all you've got. Now, I'll be honest with you. I don't believe in werewolves either. But someone, or *something*, did all this. You don't want to be out there alone tonight, Laura. You already made it clear you understand that."

"Then protect me. Give me a cell, then get out there and kill that thing."

"Okay," Robert said. "We can certainly get you a cell. Come on."

"No. I want her to take me," Laura said, nodding to Jenny. "I don't trust traitors."

Jenny looked at Robert and shrugged. "It's fine with me. Wait here, though. I need to show you something."

Robert nodded as Jenny led Laura from the room. Then, he zipped up the bag containing what was left of Robbie Atkins. Truth be told, he had no love for the boy. He'd been a menace from a young age and seemed to be on course to be worse than his father.

Robert paused at Joe's bag. They had been on opposite sides of the law ever since he joined the force, but Joe was a big part of his life as a kid. It was hard to let go of that entirely. Robert leaned in and whispered, "I'll keep her safe, old friend. I promise." He zipped the bag up.

A minute or so of eerie silence crawled by until Jenny returned to the room. "I told her we'd see about getting a doctor out to look over her arm," she said.

"Probably a good idea."

"So. You and Joe Atkins, huh?"

Robert sighed. "We went to school together. Truth be told, he was always the Joe Atkins you know to some degree or another. He got away with a lot of it because it was the 80s. Some things were okay to say back then, you know?"

"Some things were never okay to say, Rob."

"Less frowned upon, then. He definitely got worse after he was laid off. I think, to a point, he just couldn't accept that he'd voted Thatcher, and so the closures were in part his own doing. So, he ramped up his pre-existing prejudices as a way to shift the blame for his problems away from himself. I tried to be understanding, but I have limits. And you're right, the way he viewed certain people was never okay. I think we all knew it; we just didn't do anything about it. I finally stepped back a few years after Robbie was born. I haven't actually spoken to Joe in anything other than a professional capacity for ten years or so."

"Yet you still don't hate the guy."

"Of course I don't hate him. This may sound hard to believe, but he wasn't entirely bad. It's his choices that were bad."

"Don't hate the sinner, hate the sin." Jenny sighed. "Rob, you believe Tess is a woman, right?"

"Yeah. I mean, of course I believe it. Why?"

"Well, a lot of people don't. And when we marched on Parliament to defend her rights, do you know who marched in the counter-protest?"

Robert glanced down at the bag next to him. "Joe Atkins."

"And his kids. They were yelling some real nasty stuff there, Rob. And I don't mean just at the group as a whole. I mean they got right up to the three of us and told us *exactly* what they think we want to do to kids." Jenny shook her head and fixed Rob with a tired stare. "See, the thing is, on some level, being able to hate the sin makes you a good person. But for those of us that have had to fight and claw for every right we have, it comes across like you don't hate the sinner because you simply don't care enough about the bigger picture. And I'm not saying you can't find compromise or understanding with people with opposing viewpoints here. I'm just saying that some people are never gonna be good people."

Robert paused, his eyes drifting back to Joe's body again. "You seemed to deal with Laura okay."

"Oh, I still hate her. I'm just capable of being professional. And I can guarantee you the only reason she didn't recognise me today is because hate like that is blind. It's always just a means to let out all the stuff they know they can't say out loud. So, they throw out words like 'groomer' instead and paint themselves as heroes standing up to scum."

"And knowing that I don't hate them. Does that make you hate me?"

"No. Like I said, you're a good person. If it came down to it, I know you'd fight for me and my loved ones, and I can't think of a better person to have my back. I just wish you'd step out of your personal bubble a bit here, because those sinners that you don't hate sure as hell don't love you."

Robert looked at Jenny, studying her face. He blinked and shook his head, unable to find the right words.

Jenny flashed him a sad smile. "And that right there, Rob, is part of your problem. You don't want to accept what's right in front of you. Anyway. We need to get back to work." She pulled out a couple of photos and spread them over the table. "These are photos I took of the bodies. A couple at the scene and a couple here. Remember what Laura said about something using its teeth to inflict a lot of the damage? Well, there are definite teeth marks around those areas."

Robert frowned and tapped a photo showing some deep indents alongside the shallower marks. "What are these?"

"That's the thing, Robert. Laura may not have been entirely wrong. I'm not saying she was attacked by a werewolf, but these teeth marks *are* more canine than human. The pattern is wrong, though."

"What do you mean?"

"I looked it up. Let's say they were attacked by a wolf. The bite marks would look like this, but the shape would be longer. These aren't set out like a wolf's snout would be."

"Okay, so what else would make marks like this?"

"My first thought was a bear. That would explain the shorter arc. The problem there is that bears have fewer teeth. So, the number of indents is more indicative of a wolf, but the shape is somewhere in between bear and human. Then, there's these."

Jenny set out another group of photos. "I took these up at the scene. A lot of the prints were messed up. Whatever was up there moved about a lot. They look canine, though. Just big."

Robert scratched his head. "Okay. So, we're looking for a *big* animal, then. We should probably get an expert in for that."

Jenny nodded. "Given the potential size of this thing, I'd recommend calling Larry back in too."

"I did call him," Robert replied, pulling his radio out. He pressed the transmit button and said, "Larry, this is Robert. Did you get my last message?"

Silence.

Robert tried again. "Larry. Are you on your way back to the station?"

Still nothing.

Robert sighed. "He's probably just knocked the radio onto silent again. Still, I'll check where he is with the tracker and go grab him. Are you okay to make the call to the mainland? Maybe they can send someone up with the team coming to collect the bodies."

"Sure. I should probably call Tess and Mell again, too. Whatever this is, I have a feeling the sleepover shift is going to get extended."

Robert smiled. "I still don't get how you can do that. Don't you get jealous?"

"Of course not. We all have weird work shifts, so we end up like this where there are just two of us quite a lot. It makes the times when all three of us are together that much more special. Besides, what's better than loving one person and having them love you back?"

"Loving two people and having them love you back," they said in unison.

Robert chuckled. "I can barely keep up with one."

"She's still not talking to you, huh?" Robert shook his head. "You know, you may have to let her go. I don't want to drag old stuff up again, but you aren't exactly blameless in that."

"I know. Maybe when this is all over, I'll try one more time to fix it. Maybe. It can't hurt, right?" Robert stood up, suddenly feeling a bit older than he had when the night began. "Okay.

Good talk, Inspector Gill. You chase up the body pickup and try to get some animal control out here, and I'll go save Larry from whatever mess he's got himself into. Back in a bit."

"Stay safe out there, Superintendent. And, hey. At least think about what I said, yeah?"

Robert nodded and left the room.

CHAPTER EIGHT

MAGGIE BAKER FLIPPED THE SIGN ON THE FRONT DOOR, signalling that the store was finally closed for the evening. It had been a surprisingly good day. Customers trickled in steadily, each with their own tales to tell. Days like this made it easier to not shut the whole thing down.

"Ah, if only I could afford to," she said to herself. "State pension buys the bread, but not the butter."

Maggie tidied a couple of tins on the shelf opposite the counter, pulling out the odd older one with a use by date of today. She added them to the small cardboard box she'd labelled 'fox food.' If there was one thing she didn't like, it was waste. Another was starving animals. This would resolve both.

The sound of a bin being turned over rang out from somewhere outside the back of the store. Maggie smiled. "Somehow, they always know." She picked up the box, walked past the counter, nudged the door open with her elbow, and entered the small backroom.

Part of her registered the unopened stock boxes stacked in the corner, and she shook her head. At this point, it was a toss-up between laziness and lack of business that was to blame for the tight plastic wrapping still holding the tins in place. Which made today's takings all the better. Running the store wasn't going to make her rich, but it was an adequate top up.

Another bump against the bin outside pulled her back to the task at hand.

Maggie pushed the back door open and stepped out into the night. Sure enough, the old steel bin was on its side, its contents spilling over the ground "You must have figured out by now that there's nothing good in that thing," Maggie said. "You knock it over every couple of nights, and there's never any food in there."

She placed the box on the ground and picked up a tin of Irish stew. "So, you didn't like Fred," she said, lifting the ring pull, and emptying the contents into a metal dish by the door. "So, let's try something different. How about, 'Red Toast?' If you're happy with Red Toast as a name, come and get the grub."

Maggie waited, and when no fox came trotting into view, she shrugged and grabbed a tin of sweetcorn. She emptied the contents into the dish and said, "Well, suit yourself. I'll have to come up with a different name for you."

The quiet *tap, tap* of paws on stone caused Maggie to pause. She smiled and looked up, saying, "Or maybe Red Toast is the perfect—"

A tall creature stalked towards her, its eyes burning with hate, and fur bristling. Its overlong teeth would be comical were they not so threatening. They sat in a canine-like jaw that was set slightly askew as though it had been dislocated then shoved back in place. A low, guttural growl vibrated from its mouth, the sound a slow staccato of a death march.

One word whispered in the back of Maggie's head.

Werewolf.

That emboldened Maggie, somehow. She refused to be paralysed with fear. Even as her legs shook, and her heart jumped, she forced herself to stand up, step back through the door, and slam it shut.

She ran through the back room as fast as she could. The moment her feet found the main store, the door behind her exploded inward, the wood shattering as it came off the hinges. Maggie slammed the next door shut behind her and turned the manual lock, trying to buy herself a little more time. She grabbed the store phone and hit the speed dial for the police station, then took a kitchen knife from the hanging bar above it, ignoring the repeated, hard *thuds* against the rapidly cracking wood.

"Loughby police station," a voice said at the end of the line.

Before Maggie could respond, the door gave way and crashed to the floor, accompanied by a triumphant howl. The space behind the counter was limited, which Maggie hoped would slow the thing as it came at her. When it stepped into the well-lit room, though, she realised it was scrawnier than she thought, even with its height.

Maggie had seen enough conflict in her life to know not to back down. She'd been involved with protests that had turned violent. She'd fought off a thug that tried to rob her in broad daylight. And she would fight this thing too.

"Maggie Baker does not run from fucking werewolves," she yelled and swung the knife outward.

The werewolf withdrew to avoid the swipe and followed through too quickly for Maggie to get a second chance. It lashed out and sent her sprawling over the counter and into the shelf of cheap alcohol, bringing the bottles down with a crash.

Maggie had not felt pain like this before. Her leg was broken, and when she saw the beast crawl over the counter to meet her, she knew the clash wasn't going to go her way.

But she was also very stubborn. So, she grabbed a broken bottle of knock-off whisky and waited for the werewolf to bring its face towards hers. It let out a hiss-like snarl, and the smell of blood filled Maggie's nose. She pulled her own lips back to match the monster's expression and yelled, "Go to hell you miserable piece of sh—"

Just below its sparse fur, Maggie caught sight of a familiar set of scars running down the thing's arm that cut off both her words and her swing towards the monster's face. They weren't straight lines like most self-harm marks. They spelt the words 'fuck up'. That made them distinct, but that was the point. They'd been made to remind the recipient of how far he'd fallen, and their angry red colouring stood out even more against the creature's grey flesh than they did when Maggie had helped patch them up.

Maggie's eyes went wide, and she said, "Dougie?"

A clawed hand found her head, and she said no more.

Chapter Nine

"STAY SAFE OUT THERE," JENNY SAID AND GAVE THE VAN a tap.

"Will do, Inspector. Once we've got anything to report, we'll be in touch," the man in the front passenger seat replied.

"Cheers, boys." Jenny stepped back and watched the van pull out, carrying the bodies of the Atkins family towards the dock, so they could be taken to the mainland for storage and examination. She was about to re-enter the station when the rapid *pat-pat-pat* of two people running down the street caught her attention. One of them she recognised. "You're in a hurry, Selwyn," she called out.

As the big Irishman came closer the fear on his face became clearer. Selwyn regularly showed a lot of emotion. Usually happiness. Occasionally sadness, around certain times of the year. She had never seen him like this. He was also cradling his left hand.

Jenny moved to meet the two men. "Jesus Christ. What happened?"

"I was attacked," Selwyn replied. "Tom here saved me."

Jenny narrowed her eyes. "Tom. You're the guy that got dropped off earlier?"

"Yeah," Tom replied, sucking in air every couple of words. "But we…don't have time…we need help."

"Come with me," Jenny said, leading them into the station. She smiled when she caught Constable Barnes recoil at the sight of Selwyn's hand. It looked bad, but not that bad. Barnes was fresh out of training, though, and came straight to Loughby. He wouldn't have seen anything worse than a couple of cuts and bruises from minor scuffles at the Kestrel before now.

Jenny led them to an interview room and pointed them to a couple of chairs. She hit record on the audio recorder and asked, "So, what happened to the hand, Selwyn?"

"Tom hit it with a crowbar."

"Saving him," Tom added. "From that…that thing."

"Okay," Jenny said, locking her fingers and creating a rest for her chin. "When you say 'thing,' what are we talking about here?"

"A monster," Tom said.

Jenny dropped her hands to the table and tilted her head. "What happened?"

"I saw what I thought was a large fox out by my place," Selwyn said. "I went out to feed it, but it wasn't a fox."

"What was it?"

Selwyn shook his head. "It stood up, Jen. It stood up and charged straight at me."

"I saw it out the window," Tom cut in. "I ran out and grabbed the crowbar and hit it in the head. I didn't mean to hit Selwyn's hand, too."

"It's okay, lad," Selwyn said. "It ran off after that."

"Selwyn. What was it?" Jenny asked again.

Selwyn looked away, his eyes narrowing in confusion. "It looked like…it looked like a werewolf."

Jenny picked at her lower lip. "You know what? The Doc's down checking on someone in the cells. You two wait here, and I'll send him in to have a look at your hand. Do either of you want a drink?"

They both shook their heads, so Jenny stood up and said, "I'll be back."

That's two werewolf reports, she thought. *What the hell are we dealing with?*

When Jenny reached the cells, Doctor Goldblatt was sitting on the bench outside the main door. He smiled and said, "Well, I don't normally appreciate out-of-hours calls, but that was certainly something."

"How was she?"

"Hmm…I wouldn't say pleasant. Angry. Standoffish. She did, just about manage to stop a slur slipping out. With her family's reputation, I'm sure that was a challenge for her. The wound wasn't as deep as it looked, though. I cleaned it and dressed it but advised her to go to A&E on the mainland to have it stitched. She didn't seem too fond of the idea of leaving the station."

"No, I suppose she wouldn't. She lost her father and brother tonight."

"Ah, I see."

Jenny sighed and nodded back up the hall, indicating to Doctor Goldblatt that she wanted him to follow her. He rose to his feet. "Anyway, I have another one for you."

"Oh?"

"Selwyn Bonner. Got his hand cracked with a crowbar. Looks broken to me."

"Then, that's also a hospital job."

"I know. But, all things considered, I'm not sure it's a good idea anybody tries leaving the island tonight."

Doctor Goldblatt stopped and stared at Jenny. "And why would that be?"

"Nothing to worry about. It sounds like we have a wild animal running around attacking people. It's just safer to stay inside for now, that's all."

"And did this wild animal have anything to do with Miss Atkins' bereavement?"

"I'm afraid so. I'd appreciate it if you didn't spread that

around, though. We wouldn't want to cause a panic."

Doctor Goldblatt nodded, and the pair headed towards the interview rooms. As they drew close, Constable Barnes came running into view. "Inspector Gill," he yelled. "We've, uhm… something happened."

Jenny opened the door to Interview Room Two and directed Doctor Goldblatt inside. Then she turned back to the rookie and said, "Okay, Constable Barnes. What appears to be the problem?"

"We had a strange call come in. It was Maggie Baker, calling from the store. The thing is, she wasn't talking on the phone, really. She was yelling in the background." He paused and scratched his head. "It was weird. She was saying something about a werewolf."

"A werewolf," Jenny repeated, slowly. "Constable Barnes, I know this sounds like a prank call, and it wouldn't be Maggie's first, but we need to get someone out there."

"That's the problem," he replied. "I did send someone out there. Constable Ghosh. She just radioed back in. It doesn't sound good."

"In what way, not good?"

"She said it's a mess over there. Maggie's dead."

Jenny's brow furrowed involuntarily. If whatever this was was attacking people inside as well as outside, it needed to be dealt with far quicker. She placed a hand on the young Constable's shoulders and said, "Alright. Get back to the desk, and I'll go check it out."

Constable Barnes nodded and did as he was told.

Jenny leaned her head into Interview Room Two. "Listen, guys, I need to go deal with something. Do me a favour and stay here, okay? All three of you."

CHAPTER TEN

ROBERT GLANCED OVER AT SELWYN'S PLACE AND CONSIDERED letting him know that something dangerous was running around. His light was still on, so he'd still be awake. As long as he was inside, though, he was safe enough. Getting Larry was more important. Given his position on the map, it was clear that Larry had stopped in to see Dougie. That he hadn't radioed anything in meant he was safe, too. Probably.

"Most likely Dougie was drunk again," Robert mumbled to himself. "Larry heard my last call and decided to stick with him to keep him out of trouble."

He continued past the house and through to what used to be the property's garden. Selwyn had taken the fences down after Frank died, and Robert had helped him dig up the flower beds, cut down the bushes, and re-turf the area. Not because he thought it was a good idea, but because he understood that Selwyn was grieving. Now, he just had one solitary flower bed by the big window.

"Damn shame," he said. "Frank did a great job out back."

He walked on toward the trees and found his hand going instinctively to his baton, checking it was there. Something was telling him to be sure. He wasn't afraid, but given the situation, knowing his first line of defence was at hand was not a bad thing. The torch also helped.

Dougie's Castle was in a clearing about a hundred metres through the wooded area. It was built on a small plot of land that Selwyn had bought after he'd met Dougie and spoken to a few members of the community that had known him in better days. You wouldn't think it if you didn't know him, but Dougie *had* been appreciative of that. Truth be told, Dougie and Selwyn were fairly close. They argued like brothers but kept their distance a bit more.

Once the building came into view, Robert frowned. There were large holes all over what was essentially Dougie's front yard. The lights were also off. Robert pulled his phone out and checked the GPS tracker for Larry's radio. It was definitely here somewhere. He put the phone back in his pocket, pulled out the radio, and pressed the transmit button. "Larry, where are you?"

Robert heard his own voice echo somewhere up ahead. He tried again. "Larry?"

The sound drew his attention to one of the holes.

Robert put the radio away, drew his baton, and extended it to its full length. Slowly, he walked towards the hole, his grip tightening on the weapon as he angled the torch into the pit. He peered in, and the grip loosened again. The baton dropped to the floor, and Robert fell to his knees.

Larry's head had been smashed against the stone in the bottom of the hole, his features crushed into a pulp. The back of his neck had been torn open, and the spine pulled partially through. His body was crumpled to the side, bent out of shape, and partially ripped apart. Robert wanted to look away, but he couldn't. Even after seeing the Atkins family, he was still in a state of disbelief about the carnage. Then, his torch caught something on the floor.

Paw prints.

Robert stood up and scanned the area. The prints had come around from the other side of the shed, and you could see where they intersected with boot prints that he assumed belonged to Larry. Something about them felt wrong, though. They were too large, that was clear, but that wasn't it. There was something else that he couldn't quite put his finger on.

"Rob?" Inspector Gill's voice came through the radio.

Robert took a deep breath and replied, "I'm here."

"You need to get Larry, and get back here. I think things are going to get a lot worse."

Robert paused for a moment, then said, "Larry's dead."

Silence, then, "Fuck. Maggie Baker is dead too. She was attacked by…something. She called it in, sort of, and said it was… well…a werewolf. We also have Selwyn and Tom at the station. They said they were attacked by a werewolf, too. I think we might have a real problem here."

"You're not fucking kidding."

"No, I mean, I'm looking at the CCTV footage in Maggie's shop right now. It's not a great angle, but you see enough. I think… you need to see this for yourself."

"Okay. Transfer a copy of the footage to your phone and get back to the station. I'll be back there as soon as I can. Given the circumstances, I think we're gonna have to leave Larry here for the time being."

"Where is he?"

"Up outside Dougie's place."

"Dougie's place? On the video, Maggie said Dougie's name. Do you think you could have a look around before you head back? Maybe he's wandering around in a weird costume or something."

Robert glanced back towards Dougie's shed and said, "Sure. Listen, it may be a good idea to make sure everyone is inside. We don't want to cause a panic, but if we let people know there's a wild animal on the loose, we should at least limit how many people run into it."

"Okay. I'll get Barnes and Ghosh on it."

Robert turned and walked carefully to the shed. The light

wouldn't come on, so he relied on his torch to check the inside. The place was messier than Dougie usually kept it. What drew his attention, though, were the items on his desk.

One quick look was enough to get Robert worried. He stared at the illustration on the open page and something in his brain clicked. The paw marks weren't spread out like an animal's would be. They were spread out like they were made by something walking on two legs.

He grabbed the book and some of the papers and started running back towards the town.

Chapter Eleven

PAT THORPE PUSHED HIS GLASSES UP HIS NOSE AND DID HIS
best impression of a smile. It was the sort of smile that sober
people described as 'don't-ever-fucking-do-that-again level of
creepy.' Drunk people tended to go wide eyed and stumble slowly
backwards until they thought he couldn't see them anymore. As
long as they ordered something *and* paid for it, either response
was acceptable.

But, he had to smile, regardless. His therapist made that very
clear because, by his own admission, if he didn't smile away the
annoyance, he'd kick something that was not only undeserving
but would likely hurt him in the process. The moment Constable
Ghosh came in and let him—and everyone else in the pub—
know there was a wild animal on the loose, the cries for a lock-in
kicked in.

In a way, this was a pain in the arse, because it meant he'd be
working through the night. Or at least working through until
the police took care of things. At the same time, though, he had
a lot of surplus stock that was on the brink of being ditched. He
was going to make damn sure he shifted the lot of it during the
festivities.

"The idiots don't realise that someone must have gotten hurt or worse for the police to be calling for people to stay inside," he muttered, wiping a glass down behind the bar. "I wonder who it was."

"Oi, Pat," Benny Salt called. Benny was one of the Kestrel's regulars; he was a short, vaguely log-shaped man that was as annoying as he was affable. "Same again for me and Chloe, yeah?"

Pat gave the pair a curt nod and pulled them both a pint of cheap ale. He made sure Benny got the half-wiped glass as it was his order that prevented Pat from cleaning it fully. Plus, it was also Benny's blood stain that still sat defiantly on the carpet as an apparently immortal reminder of the Dougie Walters Dart Incident. Both were good reasons for him to put up with a bit of dirt in his drink.

"Hey! I didn't know lock-in meant locking the booze away," someone else yelled from the other end of the bar.

Pat turned and started to sink into an even-angrier-than-normal state, but Lianne pushed past him with a cheery, "I'm on it."

He was actually fairly grateful that she'd agreed to stick around. And on her regular pay rate, too. In what was an uncharacteristically kind moment, he decided to let the popular barmaid keep the tips for the evening.

Bang-bang-bang.

Pat glanced towards the back door, then to Lianne. "Too busy to notice," he muttered. "It's not like wild animals knock on doors. It's probably Dougie."

Bang-bang-bang.

"Fuck me, I need a smoke." Pat sighed and pulled out his tobacco tin.

Bang-bang-bang.

"Alright, I'm coming," Pat called. He walked through the door at the back of the bar, through the kitchen, and over to the back door without stopping. The cigarette was rolled, lit, and in his mouth before he even turned the knob to let the late-night caller in.

"I've told you not to come to the back door," he said out loud, masterfully bouncing the cigarette between his lips as he spoke. "Stop messing around and get out here, Dougie. The only reason I'm letting you in at all right now, is because the police want me to keep everyone inside."

Pat was met with silence. He took a big drag of the happy stick and immediately started coughing. Once he was sure he'd stopped, Pat looked at the burning roll-up between his fingers. "Fucker," he said and put it back in his mouth again. "Dougie, if you don't get in here right now, you can stay barred. I don't care if there is a wild animal out here."

A low, guttural sound came rolling in through the shadows. It wasn't exactly human, but it wasn't really *not* human either. Pat pushed his glasses up and squinted into the darkness, looking for any sign that Loughby's mysterious wild animal was just some pillock running around scaring people.

Claws scraped against cobblestones, but he turned too late towards the sound when a large hand wrapped itself around his throat. Claws dug into his flesh and lifted him off his feet. Soulless eyes bore into his and, to his shame, a hot wetness spread below his belt as his bladder emptied.

Pat's lips moved but the only sound that came out was a stuttered chatter of nonsense syllables. His eyes drifted downward, and his brain went into panic mode. A skinny, elongated arm held him several feet off the floor. The thing's feet were once human. He could see the stretch marks where it had grown out into digitigrade style. It was also very clearly male. Pat's brain whispered words of death to him, and a noise somewhere between a laugh and a cry escaped his lips.

With a snarl, the creature forced its way through the door and threw him backwards.

Pat hit part of the kitchen counter. Pain shot through his back. In a way, it was enough to force him to focus. The slightest movement sent flashes of lightning through his body, but he knew he had no time think about the pain, or even what he was going to do. Now his mind was clear again, it was time to act, not think.

He turned and scrambled to his feet, barely rising to three-quarters of his height as he made it back into the bar. He didn't even get the chance to warn everyone before the creature grabbed him and forced him forward. A short, sharp impact hit Pat's chest, and he looked down to see that the tap for one of the cheap ales was now sticking through him. All the way through him if the sudden wetness on his back was anything to go by.

For a brief moment, Pat noticed the screaming coming from all around him. Everybody was abandoning him to escape. Even Lianne was pushing ahead of the drunks to try get the front door unlocked. Not that she'd be able to. He had the only key. That wasn't the worst of it though. Just as the creature's teeth closed around the back of his head, Pat realised that the tap was for his least favourite of the Kestrel's stock.

"Why did it have to be Loughby Espresso Ale?" he grumbled and let the darkness take him.

Chapter Twelve

ROBERT ENTERED THE POLICE STATION TO FIND IT LOOKING deserted. He placed the papers he'd gathered from Dougie's shed behind the main counter and was about to start checking rooms when the sound of growing screams began to pour in from down the road. Jenny ran out from the hallway and joined him. "What the fuck is going on?" he asked.

"I have no idea."

"Any luck with animal control?"

"None. They aren't available until tomorrow."

Robert drew his baton and said, "Bastards. Come with me." A click from behind made him stop. "Jenny, what are you doing?"

She checked the cocked Glock 17 and replied, "With all due respect, Rob, you haven't seen this thing."

"There's still protocol—"

A window breaking and an increase in screaming cut off Robert's words. It was now clear that the sounds were coming from The Kestrel's Crown, a little way up the road. Several people were clambering through the broken window, following the path of the cheap chair that had skidded into the road. In a flash, a large shape dove through on top of someone who was part way out the window but struggling with the sharp glass shards still stuck to the frame.

The shape dragged the man to the floor and went straight to his leg, sinking its teeth in. The man screamed. Under the streetlights, Robert could see what Jenny meant now. Even crouched, the monster was huge. No wonder everyone cried werewolf.

It wasn't like the ones from the movies, not the famous ones. In a way, it was like it was like a partially finished costume or a rough work-in-progress design for a cheap movie. Only one thing was missing.

"It doesn't have a tail," Robert muttered.

"What?" Jenny hissed.

"We need to get its attention."

"On it." Jenny discharged a round into one of the storage crates next to the station, the *bang* of the gun lingering longer than the thud of the bullet.

The creature stopped and stood up, dragging the man into the air by the leg in its mouth. It stared at the two police officers, seemingly oblivious to the screams of the man whose leg was barely still attached to the rest of his body.

"It's Benny Salt," Jenny whispered. "Now what?"

The monster spat Benny out and ran towards them.

"We get it in the station where we're not going to hit anyone else," Robert said, moving back towards the main doors. Jenny joined him, and, once inside, she pushed herself against the wall farthest from the right. Robert, meanwhile, turned and stood facing the entrance, baton in hand. He kept his eyes straight ahead and said, "You get a shot, you don't worry about me. You take it. Understood?"

"Yes, sir," Jenny said firmly.

A dark shape loomed in the doorway. The red of its eyes was barely visible behind the frosted glass, but they were clearly fixed on Robert. For a moment, it just stood there, staring.

The creature broke forward, shoving the door aside. Robert barely had time to raise his baton before it was on him, pushing him to the floor. He got an arm up under its chin, forcing its head away from his face and allowing him to get a good look at the rage-filled, black and red eyes of the monster. As he tried to push it away, he simply redirected its attack to his shoulder.

Robert cried out as the teeth sunk into his flesh. Hearing his own voice make those sounds created a strange disconnect from his brain, like he was sliding out of his own body. Yet, the angry ragged breaths of the creature were louder. It snapped its head from side to side with every exhale; trying to force a chunk away from his shoulder was louder, though. As was the half-rip, half-crack sound of his body resisting the assault.

A loud *bang* was followed instantly by a wet *thud*, and the beast lurched into him. Oddly, the act of it removing its teeth from his shoulder hurt more than the thrashing. He watched as the thing stood up, offering barely more than a passing glance at the new wound in its arm.

The monster lunged towards Jenny, biting out a barrage of malice-fueled screeches. One, two, three shots were fired from her Glock as she took a careful step towards it. The creature stopped in its tracks then stumbled forward, barely stopping itself from dropping. It growled and advanced again. Two more shots, two more steps. The monster dove forward, catching Jenny hard enough to send her sprawling back against the wall.

Robert tried to get to his feet, but he knew he was too slow to help.

The werewolf—there was no sense denying that's what it was now—scurried forward on all fours, and Jenny discharged three more rounds. The third stray bullet hit the light and plunged the room into semi-darkness. The fourth shot caught it, though, forcing a pained, fearful wheeze of a snarl from its throat.

Panic setting in, Robert scrambled forward, grabbed it by the leg, and pulled. It twisted like a dog play fighting with its owner, then swung a hard claw at Robert, batting him away with terrifying ease.

That distraction gave Jenny enough time to sit up and take aim. Five shots rang out in quick succession, and the beast finally hit the ground. Somehow, though, it still breathed well enough to turn its malformed head towards Jenny and let out a defiant roar. Jenny took aim and fired the last rounds in the magazine into its skull, sending it into silence.

Robert forced himself up onto his knees and looked down at the body in front of him. The black and red eyes were somehow still angry, even in death. Then, the colour melted away from them, and a thick black smoke ran off its face. For a moment, Robert could have sworn it moved across the room and hovered over his damaged shoulder before slipping away, but something else distracted him. He frowned. "They're green."

"What?" Jenny asked.

"His eyes are green." Robert, hoping that was a coincidence, grabbed the werewolf's right arm and brushed the sparse hair aside. The greyish skin had sagged a little, but the scars were still vibrant. Robert had seen the same cuts the night he answered Maggie Baker's call about Dougie Walters self-harming in her shop. He dropped the arm and shook his head. "It really is Dougie."

Jenny crawled forward and checked the scars. Then she looked away, her face deep in thought. When she met his eyes again, she was wearing a look of concern. "Are you okay?"

"Do I look okay?"

She shook her head. "No, I mean, you've seen werewolf movies before, right?"

Robert shrugged and immediately had to grip his injured shoulder. "Of course I have."

Jenny nodded to the shoulder wound.

"Shit," Robert grunted. "Is the doc still here?"

Jenny nodded and dashed into the main hallway. Moments later, she returned with Doctor Goldblatt. Selwyn and Tom appeared to have come along, too. "This does not look good," the doctor said as he pulled the tear in Robert's shirt aside, visibly fighting not to look at the monstrous corpse.

Selwyn and Tom had no such inhibitions and moved past him to look down at the body. Selwyn gripped his bandaged hand, wincing at the action. "Yeah. That's what attacked me. No, wait, the eyes are different."

"While it was alive, they were black with red," Jenny said. "Look closely. It's Dougie."

Selwyn screwed his face up in disbelief. "That's impossible."

"I took some stuff from Dougie's place," Rob said. "They're behind the desk. Maybe they can explain what's going on."

Somewhere down the hallway, someone screamed.

"Fuck! It's Laura!" Robert pushed himself to his feet. He made it to the door of her cell and fumbled the keys until he found the right one. Robert opened the door just in time to see a large shape made of black smoke rise up in front of the terrified girl and dive into her, flowing into her body through every gap it could find. The majority of the smoke went straight for her wounded arm. It seeped in through the dried blood, forcing the flesh apart, re-opening the gashes, and smothering the blood in black ash.

Still, she screamed and began to thrash about. Robert tried to grab her, to keep her from hurting herself, but she threw him off and started ripping at her clothes. "I can feel it inside me! It's like fire!"

The rest of the group made it to the door and, after a brief glance into the room, tried to pull Robert towards the hallway. He pushed them back and went to Laura again. Once more, she forced him away, this time using hot, sinuous hands that pulsed as her muscles twisted and expanded in her body. Forced cries cut through laboured, irregular breaths, as the girl lowered her head and watched wide-eyed as new, sharp claws forced their way through her fingertips, ripping the old nails from her flesh.

Her teeth had begun to grow out, and some parts crumbled away as they reformed into sharp, flesh-tearing fangs. Dark ginger hair sprang from her now naked body—her natural hair colour— thicker than the hair Dougie had grown. She collapsed to the ground and writhed in agony as the change continued to rack her body.

Robert remained frozen in place, gasping as Laura's feet stretched to an unnatural length, each stuttering growth accompanied by the sound of bones breaking and reforming. Steam rose from the toes as they began to fuse together, the flesh bubbling as they became more canine in shape. Her face grew outward, creating a snout. Each spurt of growth was accompanied by a loud *crack* as her skull shifted and reformed within her. Much like the hair, it was longer than Dougie's and more in line with what Robert pictured when he thought of werewolves.

Laura's skin greyed as everything began to settle into place. Her flesh had been stretched to its limit but held strong. While Dougie had seemed like his skin could tear at any moment, Laura's was different. If anything, the tightness of it felt *efficient*. It was like her body had adapted, somehow.

Finally, the black smoke rose into Laura's eyes and solidified into a thick, black film. The girl's irises turned red, and the screaming stopped.

Laura began to slowly rise to her feet, keeping her eyes on Robert.

"All of you, run," Robert commanded and charged forward.

Chapter Thirteen

TOM RAN, KEEPING PACE WITH THE POLICE OFFICER THAT HAD briefly spoken to him and Selwyn earlier. Jenny, Selwyn had said her name was. A loud thud echoed behind him. Tom turned his head long enough to see Superintendent Cole slump down against the wall opposite Laura Atkins' cell, his head snapped to the side. Within seconds, the monster that had been a girl was on the dead man, viciously ripping through his flesh with her teeth.

Tom forced himself to look away and keep pushing forward. Jenny led them down a corridor that ended with a single door. She shoved it open and beckoned them inside. "Someone help me with the tables."

Tom grabbed a small, circular table and carried it to the door, flipping it on its side. Selwyn passed him another, and he stacked it while Jenny rearranged them, wedging them together. Once the three tables were in place, the six chairs came next.

Tom collapsed against the mass of furniture and took the room in. It was a lunchroom with a small kitchen at the back. There wasn't a huge amount of space. One thing struck him immediately. "We just blocked the only exit."

"I know," Jenny replied. "We also blocked the only entrance."

Something hard collided with the door, the impact causing the tables to shudder behind Tom. A hair-covered arm reached between the small gap the impact had created. Tom grabbed the first thing he could reach, an old trophy for something, and started slamming it into the arm until it retreated.

There was no respite. A round of loud bangs rang out from the other side of the door.

Jenny pushed her shoulder against the mass. "Selwyn, give me a hand."

The big Irishman didn't hesitate. The force of each blow visibly vibrated through both Selwyn and Jenny, but they kept pressed tightly against the wood, trying to stop the door from opening.

"This won't hold forever," Selwyn grunted.

The banging continued, getting progressively more frequent, though noticeably weaker as it went along. Eventually, it stopped, and Jenny and Selwyn flopped to the floor. "It'll hold long enough to figure something out," Jenny said.

"What exactly are those things?" Dr Goldblatt asked. "Other than, apparently, Dougie Walters and Laura Atkins."

A silence hung in the air. Tom said plainly, "Werewolves. They're werewolves."

To Tom's surprise, nobody disagreed. They didn't even attempt to try to explain it away as something else. In a way, that was worse.

After a moment, Dr Goldblatt asked, "I don't suppose you have any silver bullets in that gun?"

Jenny shook her head. "No ammo at all. It didn't take a silver bullet to put Dougie down, though. It just took a lot."

"It's not a full moon either," Selwyn added, "and aren't they supposed to turn back when you kill them? What if Dougie's still alive out there? Then we've got two of them to deal with."

Tom shook his head. "Or maybe the movies were wrong about how werewolves work?"

"I think we can agree on that," Jenny said. She sighed. "Dougie's eyes changed back, though."

"So maybe that's it?" Tom tried. "The transformation is one way. Did it attack Laura?"

"She had a wound on her arm," Dr Goldblatt replied. "It looked like claw marks."

Selwyn grimaced. "And then she changed. So, the stories are right about how it passes to different people. Thank fuck Tom got my hand, not Dougie."

Jenny gave him a stern look. "That would mean Robert would have changed eventually. And any of the survivors from whatever happened at the Kestrel's Crown could, too, if they were bitten or scratched."

"Ah, shit," Selwyn said. "If it got into the Kestrel, we could be overrun."

Jenny leaned back against the table and shook her head. "No. I don't think so."

"How can you be so sure?" Tom asked.

"Because Laura didn't change until after Dougie died. There was that smoke that left his eyes, too. It sort of moved around Rob's arm a bit, but I don't think he noticed. Then, it was there when Laura changed. In her eyes, I mean. It was the last thing to happen. I think…however this works, it can only affect one person at a time. They don't heal like in the movies, either. Did you see Laura's arm when she tried to get in? It still had the claw marks on it."

"Okay, so let's grab every cop on the island and kill her." The moment the words left Tom's mouth, silence overtook the room. There was a quiet resignation on everyone's face. Given how things played out with Dougie, it couldn't end any other way. And the cycle may continue afterwards, depending on whether there were any survivors in the pub, and whether they were hurt.

Then, the fear crept into Jenny's eyes, too, and she grabbed her radio. She switched to broadcast on all channels and said, "Barnes, Ghosh, are you there?"

"Here," came the first reply from a young male voice.

"Here," followed the next, a female this time.

"Okay, listen. We have a situation here. For now, do not come back to the station. I repeat, *do not* come back to the station."

"Well, it's a bit late for that," the female voice replied. "I'm just—"

The audio cut abruptly to silence, and a muffled scream made its way down the hallway, accompanied by a barrage of short, angry roars.

"Constable Ghosh," Jenny tried. "Constable Ghosh. Come in."

No response came.

Tom bit his lip. "What about the other one?"

Jenny flopped her head back against the table and hit transmit. "Barnes, stay away. You got that?"

"What happened to Annabelle?" came the reply.

Jenny's voice was flat now. "We can assume she's gone. Superintendent Cole, too. And Constable Flanaghan. We're the only two coppers left on the island. I'm holed up in the canteen with a couple of survivors. Where are you?"

"Cross Street."

"Okay. Listen. Go to Maggie Baker's shop. *Do not* look under the cover. Trust me. Find something to arm yourself with and lay low for now. Batons aren't going to be any use here, and the spray is just going to get this thing mad."

There was a brief pause. "Inspector Gill…are we really dealing with a werewolf?"

"Forget silver. Whether this thing is a werewolf or not, you can hurt it without silver. It's just tough."

"Understood. I'm entering the shop now."

The room fell into silence again.

"So, I never did ask," Selwyn said. "What brought you to Kent, Tom?"

Tom noticed the pleading quality to Selwyn's question. He shrugged. "Just passing through."

"Come on, now, lad. You know what I mean. We may be here a little while, so we might as well break the tension a bit, yeah?"

Tom nodded. "My parents died, and I inherited the house.

I'd lived there my whole life, and, without them, it didn't feel like a home anymore. So, I sold it. I had no real plan. With nowhere else to go, I just kinda wandered about a bit, staying at hotels. The money started running low last year. I still have some, but I've been trying to keep expenses as low as possible until I find somewhere that feels like home."

"How does Loughby Island grab you?" Dr Goldblatt asked.

Tom looked up to see the old man smiling, and he chuckled. "Well, it's the most exciting place I've been."

"Do you ever stay anywhere long enough for it to start feeling familiar?" Jenny asked.

"Probably not."

Selwyn squeezed Tom's shoulder. "Grief isn't the best thing to run from. If it isn't following you, it's overtaking you and waiting to meet you where you end up next."

"For what it's worth," Jenny added, "When this is all over, you're gonna need to stick around for a bit anyway while we tidy up. You may grow to like the place."

Tom felt a small smile creep to his lips and forced it away. "It's funny. I always carry some chalk and charcoal with me. I used to love art when my parents were still around, but I just didn't have the heart to carry on once I started travelling. I figured if I ever found somewhere that looked nice enough to make me want to draw it, that'd be the place I settle. There were a couple of palaces around here that kinda made me want to get a sketchbook again."

A louder, harder bang blasted out as something hit the door. Jenny and Selwyn rose to their feet, but that moment of being disconnected from the barricade was enough for the monster to start forcing the door open.

The tables and chairs screeched as they were pushed back along the floor, and through the newly opened gap came the upper body of Constable Ghosh. It had been ripped away from its other half, and the lower jaw had been removed. Her intestines and her tongue all dangled limply and waggled from side to side as her body was shaken like a grotesque hand puppet. The sight of the mangled policewoman made everyone step back, allowing the beast to force her way through the door.

The werewolf dropped Constable Ghosh's body and grabbed a table before hurling it across the room. Dr Goldblatt took the full force and was thrown backwards against the wall. He cried out as his body crumpled, one of his legs bent the wrong way. A moment of realization hit Dr Goldblatt's face, and he passed out.

The monster advanced towards the fallen doctor but was stopped in its tracks by Jenny clattering a chair against its head. The impact did no damage, but the beast still turned towards the now-retreating officer. Tom and Selwyn grabbed her and dragged her out the door, and the three ran up the hallway towards the main entrance, the sounds of heavy footsteps following calmly behind them. As they neared their escape, the footsteps sped up. All three realised at the same time that the click of claws on tile followed by silence could only mean one thing, and they dove to the sides.

The werewolf sailed past them and landed in front of the door, blocking their exit. In the half-light, it seemed to flash its teeth in a sadistic smile. It looked from left to right, stopping briefly to watch of the now scattered trio. Finally, it stepped towards Tom.

Tom backed away, frantically looking for a way to get around it. Without warning, the doors flew open.

Constable Barnes stormed into the station and raised an aerosol can and a lighter. A stream of flame hit the back of the werewolf, causing it to howl in pain.

"Barnes!" Jenny yelled. "I thought I told you to stay put!"

"I watched the security video," he replied, shooting off short bursts to keep the werewolf moving. "I couldn't leave you all."

Tom darted around the creature while it covered its eyes. At the same time, Jenny quickly grabbed something from the main desk and signaled for the four of them to back out. Constable Barnes, ignoring her, advanced a single step, but stopped when his foot hit the wet remains of Constable Ghosh's lower body. He growled, "She'd finally agreed to go on a date with me!"

Constable Barnes let out another blast of heat and turned to join them outside the station. Just as he set one foot outside the doorway, though, the monster was on him. It slammed the young man's head against the door frame with a hard right hand. Then, it grabbed him with its left and slammed his face against the other side of the frame. And back again. And again. And again.

The sheer force kept Constable Barnes's lifeless body pressed upright against the doorframe. The beast's eyes met Tom's, and she flashed that smile again before leaning into the officer's mangled face and licking the oozing pulp that dripped to the ground.

"We need to run," Tom whispered. Moments later, the *click-clack* of claws on cobblestones matched their pace.

Tom wanted to refuse to be scared, to refuse to give it the satisfaction. But he couldn't.

Chapter Fourteen

"WE NEED TO GET HER AS FAR AWAY FROM THE TOWN AS possible, "Jenny said, leading the other survivors up the bank outside the town. "You're is the only full-size building up this way. Do you think we could lock ourselves in there?"

Selwyn looked at her, and she noticed his eyes dart behind them, briefly. "Possibly. I'm gonna guess she'll get in easy enough, though."

Jenny nodded. "Maybe. But it may give us enough time to come up with a plan or find something to fight back with. I don't suppose you have a secret gun stash in there? I promise I won't arrest you."

Selwyn chuckled. "I wish."

"What's that?" Tom cut in.

Jenny followed his eyes to the book in her hands. "I'm not sure yet. I think it's what Robert found at Dougie's place. He must have thought it was important. I'm hoping it might contain something useful."

"Do you really think that thing's gonna give us a chance to read something that thick?" Selwyn asked.

"No. But what are the odds the pages either side of where he's stuck the badly folded papers will be why he took it?"

Selwyn nodded and pushed ahead up the small hill. He pointed towards the side of his house. "We didn't stop to lock up on the way down to the station. The kitchen door should still be open."

Jenny checked over her shoulder. The thing that was Laura Atkins was still following and hadn't moved any closer at all. She was the exact same distance as she had been the whole journey. *I know she can move quicker than that*, she thought. *Which means she's matching our pace intentionally. She's trying to freak us out. She's enjoying this. But how long until she gets bored with that?* Jenny sped up, and both Tom and Selwyn followed suit.

As they neared the house, Tom dashed ahead and grabbed a crowbar from the floor. The three of them barreled into Selwyn's kitchen and shut the door behind them. Selwyn pulled the latch across, then turned toward the fridge and said, "Someone help me with this."

Tom grabbed the other side of the appliance and helped drag it in front of the door while Selwyn pushed from behind.

"Is there anything we can block the front door with?" Jenny asked.

"Sofa," Selwyn said. He dashed to the front room and dragged the seat across the floor and placed it in front of the door, then shook his bandaged hand out and let out a frustrated, "Fuck."

Jenny chucked the book onto the small coffee table and rushed over to help him wedge it into place.

"Nothing we can do with this, though," Selwyn added, walking towards the bay window. When he got there, he froze.

Jenny joined Selwyn and stared out into the darkness. About twenty meters from the house, Laura Atkins stood staring back at them. She was unmoving, and her unnaturally large teeth glistened as she watched them watching her. Jenny pulled the curtains closed and guided Selwyn back towards the armchair.

"Why isn't she trying to get in?" Selwyn asked. "The sofa might slow her, but not much. Double glazing and a curtain won't do any better."

"When he attacked you, did Dougie try to scare you?" Jenny asked. "More than he needed to?"

Selwyn shook his head. "He waited to attack, but it was more like he was watching to see what I was going to do."

"I watched the camera footage at Maggie's shop. He came in after her and made it quick. It looked like he wasn't wasting any time at the Kestrel's Crown either, and he definitely didn't want to mess around with me or Rob." Jenny let her eyes wander back to the window. "Laura is different. She's playing with her food. This is fun for her."

Tom shivered and wrapped his arms around himself. "Jesus Christ. She'll make sure we feel every moment, won't she? We're not just fucked, we're being fucking tortured."

Jenny searched Tom's eyes, trying to find the right words to calm him. To her shame, all she could manage was putting a hand on his shoulder and saying, "We're alive right now. That means we still have a chance." To her surprise, that seemed to work, at least a little.

Jenny walked over to the coffee table and opened the book. She gave the loose papers a scan and frowned. She flicked back and forth a few pages and compared the contents to the handwritten notes, noting where symbols married up. Finally, she came to an old map and a piece of acetate that, when laid on top, marked out various modern locations around the island.

"Anything useful?" Tom asked, desperation creeping into the question.

Jenny waved him and Selwyn over. She pointed to the map first, saying, "We're here, and Dougie's shed is here."

Selwyn tapped a symbol on the ripped page. "What's that next to Dougie's place?"

"I'm not sure, but it matches this," Jenny replied, moving the map out of the way to reveal an old illustration in the book. "The symbol here on…I think it's an altar?"

"That…that's definitely a werewolf, isn't it?" Tom said, staring at the trio of images under the altar. "But what about that?"

Jenny let her eyes drift up to the creature at the top of the image, and she let out an involuntary shudder. "I think Dougie was translating the book," she muttered.

Selwyn grabbed the handful of handwritten papers and started to skim over them. "It's a holy book," he said and looked down at the map again. He started tapping various points where the mishmash of lines intersected, touching the different symbols. "Look, there are a bunch of different symbols like that one."

Jenny flipped back a few pages until she found another illustration of an altar, this time showing a creature that appeared to be a mix of coiled parchment and wings. It had marks behind it that reminded her of the way Christian churches illustrated holy light on stained glass windows. At the foot of its altar, a man sat cross legged with a knife in his hand. His head was upside down, and his mouth was twisted into an evil grin. All around him were the bodies of other people.

Most importantly, on the altar itself was a clear symbol. Jenny pointed to a part of the map that coincided with one of the houses in town. "That one's here."

"Do you think Dougie translated everything up to this point?" Tom asked.

"I doubt it," Selwyn said. "This map has to be the one he got from the library, right? I'm guessing because it marks where these things, whatever they are, are supposed to be. That wasn't that long ago. I reckon he probably started with the pages that related to the area near his shed. Where he got the damn book, I couldn't tell ya."

Jenny crossed her arms. "Maybe he didn't know about it. Maybe he saw the map, realised what it was, and…the mainland said he stole a shovel. He could have been trying to dig up an old altar as an archaeological find, and this book was just buried there."

Selwyn put the papers down. "Yeah, well, it's a shame he didn't translate anything about turning someone back or killing the monsters easier. These bits are more like a summoning or something like that."

Jenny started reading them again, comparing them to the old book. "It says the lupine pestilence is passed on to by tooth and claw…there's a couple of mentions of anger and revenge…Wait, look at this page. It's got that demon thing coming out of a person's mouth and going into this circle. Maybe this is how to take the monster out of someone?"

"Did Dougie translate the page?"

Jenny turned the last of the handwritten notes over and shook her head. "Maybe there are more translated pages at the shed. We could try to-"

Jenny's words were cut off by a loud but rhythmic *bang, skrak, bang, skrak, bang, skrak* at the window. It was a slow, deliberate sound. All three looked at each other, but it was Tom that stepped forward, creeping towards the curtain. He grabbed it and cautiously started to pull it aside but leapt back when he saw what they were all expecting to be there.

Laura Atkins stood at the other side of the glass, staring a hole into Tom with her black and red eyes. She was slapping her hand against the window—not hard enough to break it but more than hard enough to make a loud sound—then scraping her claws down the glass.

"Oh, fuck," Tom squeaked, his knees shaking and buckling underneath him.

Jenny stepped forward and, for a moment, locked eyes with the monster. The rage Laura felt burned into her, and she felt the air forcing its way out of her lungs. She grabbed the curtain and pulled it closed again then turned to Selwyn and Tom and said, "Grab what you can to defend yourselves with."

Jenny strode towards the kitchen and picked up a thick, sturdy-looking knife. Then, something caught her eye. "Selwyn, what's in here?"

Selwyn entered the room and stood beside her. Seeing the knife, he took another from the same block, then followed her line of sight. "Recycling. That one's paper, then there's tin, and the last one is glass."

"I have an idea," Jenny said. "You ever watch Home Alone?"

"That one I have seen," Tom replied, joining them in the kitchen, clutching his crowbar tight.

Jenny reached into the bin and pulled out a glass bottle. She lifted it above her head then threw it against the floor by the back door, smashing it into pieces. "I say we make it really fucking uncomfortable for her to come in. This is going to be way more effective than small toys."

Tom and Selwyn didn't need to be told twice. They simply grabbed a couple of bottles and took them to the living room. Intermittently, the sound of shattering glass drowned out the banging on the window.

It wasn't long after the final bottle was smashed that the banging stopped. The silence drew all three of them together, instinctively gathering in the centre of the living room, each one watching a potential entry point.

The door in the kitchen slammed against the back of the fridge, drawing their attention. Moments later, the fridge scraped noisily against the floor, pushed aside by the force of the door. The werewolf—that's all Laura was now, there was no getting around that—stood in the doorway and looked at the weapons each person held. She started to take a step into the house but stopped when she noticed the shards of glass. She tilted her head at the sharp chunks, then glanced at the trio, curling her lip with a disdain that looked like a beaten dog imitating the master that pities it for continually coming back for more.

She squatted down, raised a hand, and slammed it into a thick pile of glass. Then, she lifted the hand up, showing the broken pieces sticking out of her now-bloodied palm and fingers. Slowly, the monster closed her hand into a fist, the glass crunching loudly as it tensed up. One of her fingers spasmed with the movement, and the monster began to salivate at the sight of her own blood dripping from between her clenched fingers.

Without warning, she withdrew back around the corner. Loud footsteps skittered around the outside of the house, all the way to the front door. A single *bang* tore through the room as the door slammed open, sending the sofa sliding into the stairs. The werewolf let out a triumphant roar-bark, and retreated to the shadows, leaving nothing but the red of her eyes to watch as Selwyn scrambled to shut the door again.

"What the hell is she doing?" Tom asked. "Did we scare her away?"

Jenny shook her head. "You saw how she reacted to the glass. She's mocking us. She's showing us that she can get in any time she wants, and she's giving us time to set up more things to amuse her."

Bang.

Jenny and Tom turned to see Selwyn standing with a balled fist against the front door. "You said it didn't take silver to kill Dougie," he said and turned his head to look over his shoulder at them. "I will not be made to feel this afraid in my own home. I say we find *everything* we can to fight that bitch, and when she comes back, we finish this."

Tom nodded and started opening drawers and cupboards. Jenny went to the kitchen and filled the kettle, setting it to boil.

"It's not the time for tea," Selwyn stated flatly.

"No," Jenny agreed, "but there isn't a person alive that enjoys a face full of boiling water."

Selwyn glanced at the broken glass on the floor and said, "Well, let's hope monsters don't enjoy it either," then headed towards the stairs.

Chapter Fifteen

BANG. BANG. BANG.

The banging on the window had returned. This time, it was less rhythmic but heavier. Each slam against the glass was beginning to feel like a gunshot in Tom's head. He was doing his best to ignore it, but it was getting harder with each impact. He sighed and returned to taking stock of what he, Jenny, and Selwyn had gathered.

Jenny picked up a cricket bat and weighed it in her hands. "Remember, if she comes at you, defend against her claws and teeth. If the book is right, that's how the curse moves on to you. While one person defends, the other two attack."

Bang. Bang. Bang.

Selwyn gripped his kitchen knife tight. "How long is she gonna keep hitting my fucking window?"

"She wants a reaction," Tom said, as much to himself as Selwyn. "Don't let her get to you. We need to stay calm."

Selwyn chuckled, but there wasn't even a hint of the jovial nature he usually projected. "Stay calm? You do realise we're gonna die tonight, don't you, lad?"

"Selwyn," Jenny began.

"No," he snapped. "You saw what she did to that other fella.

She's worse than Dougie was, and it took near enough a whole damn clip of ammo to take him down."

Bang. Bang. Bang.

"What happened to not being made to feel afraid in your own home?" Jenny asked.

"Do you think I *want* to be afraid, Jenn? I'm fucking angry. I'm willing to fight, but I'm terrified. I've got one working hand, and we're up against a werewolf. A real werewolf. Or someone possessed by a demon or a god. Laura Atkins…that family… they were always monsters. Now it's literal. And how exactly did Dougie get himself mixed up in this? What the hell was he playing at summoning that bloody thing?"

"Do you think he did it on purpose?" Tom asked, staring at the translations Dougie had made. "I mean, maybe he wanted revenge on Joe Atkins and it just got out of hand?"

Bang. Bang. Bang.

"No," Jenny said, taking the papers from Tom and studying the words. "He wasn't a religious man. Nor was he that vindictive. Quicker to anger than he once was, sure, but not driven by revenge. He was probably just reading the original text out loud to check it sounded right and had no idea it would actually do anything. And here, it says ,if no son of man who have wronged you are left, the beast will find more hate within you, magnifying even the smallest quarrel.' That's why he came for the people that he did--the Atkins family for a lifetime of torment, Larry for that stupid blood light, Selwyn for arguing with him, Maggie for refusing to sell him alcohol, Benny for goading him into throwing darts at him, and Pat for barring him from the Kestrel as a result. Me and Rob was probably just because I shot at him."

"And Laura…Laura and her family think the whole damn world wronged them. Especially those of us who have or could stop them from doing what they wanted. Or the ones they think are taking something from them, whether it be benefits, the right to be an arsehole, or whatever else they're focused on right now. Mostly, they always hated those who didn't bow down to their bullshit. We're in the firing line, just because we aren't like her. And she's a bigger monster than Dougie was because, deep down, she was always a monster."

For a moment, the banging at the window stopped. The silence went on just long enough for it to be noticeable. Jenny, Selwyn, and Tom all turned their heads.

"Is she—" Tom began, but his words were cut short by a loud crash as something smashed partway through the glass and collapsed over the sill and into the room.

Jenny yanked the curtains open while Tom and Selwyn backed up. There was no sign of the werewolf, but the sight in front of her was enough to draw an involuntary gasp from her throat. There wasn't much left of the face. It looked like it had been smashed over and over against something—presumably the window, judging by the wet *pieces* stuck to the part that wasn't broken—but the short, scruffy black hair and uniform were enough. "It's Larry," she said, her eyes fixed on the body and wide open.

"Jenn!" Selwyn yelled, but it was too late.

The beast careened around the corner at top speed and dove over the fallen cop, landing on top of Jenny. She was unable to stop the impact but managed to get her left arm up, still holding the cricket bat, and forced herself into a roll the moment she hit the floor. She landed on top of the monster and fought hard to keep her in place.

Looking on, Tom realised very quickly that all the little games the monster had been playing were nothing compared to what she was now prepared to do. Laura Atkins had been hate-filled and every piece of that hatred had been magnified by whatever was drawn in the old book. The way she looked up at Jenny. The pure, unadulterated intent behind her movements. The tensing and clenching of her exaggerated limbs, claws, and teeth. This version of Laura Atkins wasn't just hateful. She was soulless. This was a Laura Atkins born of her worst traits. A literal monster, pure and simple. And now, as much as he wanted them to, his legs just wouldn't move.

Crack.

Selwyn had charged forward and aimed a soccer punt at Laura's face. The impact snapped her head to the side but appeared to do nothing else other than anger her. In response, she growled at Selwyn then scrambled her arms free and wrapped them around Jenny's body, pulling her in tight. Laura twisted her head, trying to get her jaws around the struggling policewoman's throat. When that failed, she turned her head to the side and sunk her teeth into Jenny's shoulder and rolled over onto all fours.

Tom remained frozen in place while Jenny screamed in pain, and the werewolf's lips pulled back and up into a wide-mouthed canine grin. Saliva poured from between her teeth, mixing with the blood, and her tongue thrashed wildly at the new wound. There was glee on her face, and the realization made Tom shiver. *Come on. Get moving. Do something.*

Laura sunk her teeth in further, letting out a mocking, high-pitched roar in time with Jenny's cries. But then, Selwyn was there again, this time slamming the kitchen knife down hard, embedding it in the beast's back. She howled with rage and stood up, whipping her head upward and flinging the bleeding cop into the air, smashing the light. The sound of falling glass was joined by a *thud* as Jenny's body hit the floor. Laura advanced on the now unarmed Irishman.

Selwyn began to back up toward the kitchen.

"He was right," Tom whispered. "We're all going to die tonight." Tom gripped the crowbar tight. Finally, his body moved. "I don't want to die," he screamed as he ran up behind Laura and swung the crowbar. The swing was awkward, and rather than catching the monster in the back of the head, it wrapped around the side of her face, and the curved end caught her in the eye.

The werewolf screamed.

"See?" Selwyn growled. "You *can* be hurt, ya bitch!"

The werewolf fixed Selwyn with its one remaining eye and snarled. Then, she turned, just in time to catch Tom's crowbar as he tried a second swing. With a hard pull, she brought him closer to her muzzle. She forced the chunk of metal from his hand, threw it across the room, and grabbed him by the head, yanking it to the side so he had no choice but to look at the bloodied mess he'd left in her eye socket. He struggled to break free, but she forced him back in place and rasped out a sound somewhere between a growl and a laugh, seemingly wanting to make sure he saw the damage he had done and understand how little it meant.

Before Laura could attack, Jenny was up. She swung the cricket bat once into the back of the beast's knee, but the impact of wood on bone rattled up her arm, causing her to cry out and drop the weapon. The blow was enough to cause Laura to collapse to one knee, though, and Tom struggled free.

Selwyn grabbed the kettle and ran in, yanking the lid off and throwing the contents into the monster's face.

Again, Laura Atkins screamed.

Selwyn grabbed the cricket bat from the floor and started to swing blow after blow down onto the monster's head. It only took one blow for him to cry out and let go with his bandaged hand, but it didn't matter. Even swinging one handed, the bat hit hard. Laura buckled slightly with each impact but kept trying to push up. Five blows. Six blows. Seven. On the eighth, Laura turned her body and lunged underneath, shoving Selwyn back against the wall.

Before she could rise fully, Tom swung the crowbar again, this time aiming the curved end at her face. Laura roared defiantly, and it landed between the werewolf's teeth, burying itself in her throat. Tom had swung hard, and he had followed through. The curved point exited out of the monster's neck, just below the lower jaw.

Tom gave the crowbar a pull and hauled Laura forward. She caught herself and shoved Tom away, just in time to get one hand down to stop herself falling flat to the floor. She looked up at them and bared her teeth. Blood pooled around the metal bar, and she had to make a visible effort to force some of it out of her mouth.

Jenny stumbled out of the kitchen and dumped two bottles of cooking oil over Laura's head and body. The creature snarled again and turned towards her as she struck a match. Jenny tossed the lit stick, and the flame caught the mix of oil and fur. The monster ignited.

But the beast that was once Laura Atkins would not go quietly into the night. She attempted once more to rise to her feet, screeching in pain and rage, but Selwyn was quicker. He aimed another kick at her face, and she fell to the ground, yowling and writhing. Blood poured from around her teeth, smearing the floor with partial prints of her snout as she tossed her head from side to side, trying to regain her bearings.

Realizing this was their best shot, Tom started to stomp on the panicked beast. Jenny and Selwyn piled in too, raining down hard kicks to any part of her they could reach. Tom felt bones crack beneath the impact on a strike to ribs. He felt the monster weakly try to swat him away, saw her try to do the same to Jenny and Selwyn.

As Laura rolled onto her back, the fire now almost out, the damage was on full display. Still, the werewolf kept swinging her claws at them and snapping her teeth, albeit with far less force now. Tom walked over to the window, picked up a large piece of broken glass, and plunged it into the monster's chest. Pain surged through him as the glass cut into his hand, but he ignored it, pushing the makeshift weapon as deep as he could. "Fuck you," he whispered.

Laura Atkins let out a desperate whine that seemed to take her breath with it as her body twitched then fell still. Finally, she was silent. The red melted from her one remaining eye, forming a dark smoke that hung in the air.

"Is that it?" Selwyn asked.

"No," Jenny said. "You need to run."

The smoke whipped through the air, expanding into a large, formless shape as it dove into Jenny's open shoulder wound.

Selwyn stood back, his skin going pale as he stared in shock.

"I'm burning up!" Jenny screamed.

A single, partially formed thought struck Tom. He ran to the old book, still sat on the table at the side of the room, and started turning pages until he reached the end of the section on the *thing* that was supposedly responsible for what was happening. "The circle that pulls the thing out," he cried. "Where's my bag? I need chalk."

That seemed to snap Selwyn out of his shock, and he turned to Tom, mouthing the word as it registered. Without any further hesitation, he ran to the far wall and grabbed Tom's bag. "Do you know what you're doing?"

Tom took the bag and started rummaging through until he found the chalk. He immediately started drawing a large circle on the floor. "No. But what choice do we have?"

Selwyn nodded and went to the cop, holding her tight as she screamed and shook, the mental effort it was taking to fight the transformation clear on her face.

Tom continued to work, several intersecting lines within the circle, and copying the strange rune-like text around the outside edge. Once it was done, he turned to Selwyn and said, "Get her over here. Now."

Selwyn picked Jenny up and carried her into the circle, placing her on the floor next to Tom. She began to shudder, her flesh throbbing as she tensed her body. The change showed no sign of stopping, and within seconds, Jenny's fingernails had fallen to the ground, black claws tearing through her flesh in their place.

"Nothing's happening, lad," Selwyn said, panic dripping from every word.

"Shit," Tom said, staring at the page. "I thought it would… wait…"

Blood. It's the blood it wants, Tom realised. With a grimace, he reached over to Jenny's shoulder, and placed his hand in the wound. If it hurt her, the pain was lost to what else was happening to her body. With a cry of desperation, he slammed his bloody hand into the middle of the circle.

A hard gust of wind hit all three of them but somehow didn't disturb the salt. There was a flash of light and, suddenly, a wall of heat. They looked toward the source of the sensations and saw *it.*

Standing in the middle of the room was the thing from the book. It was well over eight feet tall, towering above them with a cold menace. For the next few seconds, that was all it did, just stare at them. Then, it bowed, bringing one arm across its middle and stopping its head at the edge of the circle. Finally, it spread its massive wings, blocking out the light from the kitchen. It pulled its arm back out to the side and faded into smoke.

Breathing heavily, Jenny looked down at her hands, studying the claws that were now part of her. Her skin was alarmingly pale, and she was shaking. "How did…" she wheezed. "You couldn't…know that…would work…"

"No," Tom said. "But if it didn't, we were dead anyway. Sorry about your shoulder. There was a picture of bloody hands under the more detailed diagram of the circle. I thought it might be a reference to people with blood on their hands, but when it didn't work, I realised it must need blood from the person you're trying to keep from changing."

"It didn't change you back though," Selwyn said.

"No, but did stop it going further. Thank you. Both of you."

Silence fell on the room, and Tom glanced over towards what remained of Laura Atkins. His eyes were drawn to the injuries he knew he'd inflicted. A rib. The eye. The mouth. He burst into tears.

"It's okay," Selwyn said, putting an arm around him. "It's over now."

"No, it's not okay," Tom said, pushing Selwyn away. "Look at what we had to do. Look at what *I* did to her. I know what she did. What she'd become. But what's the difference between sticking a fucking crowbar through someone's throat and… and…"

"The difference," Jenny replied, "is that you were fighting for your life, not to end someone else's. Fighting is never clean, Tom. There's gonna be a lot of mess for all of us to clean up. But the good guys won here. Sometimes, that matters more than what had to be done to reach that end."

Tom sat back and let the tears continue to fall. Guilt still picked at his mind, but he knew Jenny was right. He took a deep breath, closed his eyes, exhaled, and let the relief wash over him.

Straying Off The Path:
AN EXPLORATION OF
THE BEAST OF LOUGHBY ISLAND

INTRODUCTION

In *An American Werewolf in London (1981)*, David Kessler and Jack Goodman are advised to stay on the path and avoid the moors. Of course, we all know what happens when they don't heed this advice. Were the results horrific? Tragic? Yes, and yes. Without David and Jack stepping away from the expected route, though, the story would not have happened.

I like to stray from the path quite a lot with my writing. I ignore rules, both commonly accepted, and ones I've set for myself. And genre conventions? Bend them and blend them until you've got a smoothie, that's what I say. That's not because I think it's bad to build a tale on common tropes and themes. The literary world is full of stories that go exactly where you expect them to, treading well-worn paths while doing so, and are still classics. It's more that I feel the need to explore. Which brings me to this book.

The Beast of Loughby Island represents, I hope, a departure from the path for you in terms of werewolf tales. To that end, I'm using this space to talk a little about werewolf history, what changes I've made to common lycanthropic lore, and how that all fits with the themes of the book. As such, if you've jumped straight to here, you may want to hop back to the start and wait until you've read the book to continue. Or, to put it another way: There are spoilers ahead.

WEREWOLF LORE: A BRIEF HISTORY

I love werewolves. They've been my favourite monster since I was a child. Right now, I'm on a quest to own a physical copy of every werewolf movie still in existence, and my collection currently sits at a little over 100 DVDs and Blurays. Of course, there are books too. When I read the High Moor Trilogy by Graeme Reynolds, that had a huge impact on me. The three books are all very different. They mix the werewolf premise with different styles of story, yet never lose what makes them so good. When I was struggling with collecting my ideas for *The Beast of Loughby Island*, the ride Graeme's trilogy took me on inspired me to push forward and do what I'd wanted to for a long time: write a full-length werewolf story in my own style.

One thing I've taken great pride in over the years is when readers refer to my books with phrases like, "I haven't read anything like it before." Honestly, I find it fun to look at what has come before and try to add my own twist to it. So, I set about doing my thing and exploring different ways the famous monster has been presented historically. In the present day, werewolves have set rules. Generally speaking, they can usually be condensed down to this:

The curse is passed on by surviving being bitten by a werewolf.

The werewolf shifts form on a full moon.

The werewolf is vulnerable to silver.

Now, there are exceptions to each rule, of course. For example, *Ginger Snaps (2000)*, saw the curse being passed on through unprotected sex. That was a necessity for the story, because much like *Company of Wolves (1984)*, Ginger Snaps used the werewolf as a metaphor for puberty and transitioning into adulthood. If you move outside horror, Urban Fantasy novels tend to have shifts regardless of the moon phase, as that allows for some nice set pieces without having to worry about the date. There are exceptions to the silver rule too, though that one seems to be a little more sticky in terms of how werewolves are viewed.

Here's the thing though. You can attribute the popularisation of these rules to Universal Pictures. *The Wolfman (1941)*, sees Sir JoÚ Talbot being bitten by a werewolf and undergoing a change from there. He is eventually killed with a silver cane. Now, the famous poem used in the film actually stated that the change occurs during the Autumn moon. This was changed in later films to a full moon, likely as a way to bring the character back. As a result, a fair few people now think the original film mentioned the full moon too.

That is not to say that Universal Pictures made the lore up, though. There are old myths and legends that do reference all of these things to one degree or another. They just weren't hard and fast rules. The werewolf curse itself was often something someone sought out for their own gains. Sometimes, that meant acquiring magical belts that allowed the wearer to change shape. Other people performed spells or rituals, often involving things like drinking rain water from the fresh tracks of a wolf. *Wolf Blood: A Tale of the Forest (1925)* is a silent movie, and the oldest werewolf movie to not be considered lost. There, the fear of lycanthropy is attributed to an emergency blood transfusion between a man and a wolf.

Then there were deals with the Devil. During the rise of Christianity, proclaiming someone as having made a deal with a demon of some sort was a good way to make sure others feared them. For would-be werewolves, they would allegedly trade their souls for the ability to shapeshift into a wolf. Biting was not a necessity, and the curse was not something that was passed on.

As you can imagine, none of those old ways to become a furry killing machine rely on the full moon, either. Werewolves regularly shifted whenever they wanted. It was more to do with power and using that for their own goals, be that revenge or simply coveting something. Silver, too, was a mixed bag. It was used in some stories because it was pure, or in others because silver ornaments in the local church was all that was available to melt down into bullets. Fire was also very effective, though. Werewolves burned easily. Sometimes, they were just hunted down with regular weapons. It all depended on what point the story was making. Most of the werewolves of yore would not have survived being blown up like the one in *Monster Squad (1987)*, for example.

THE INTERPLAY BETWEEN LORE AND THEMES IN THE BEAST OF LOUGHBY ISLAND

I wanted to create a lore that was a mix of old and new elements, including a few from outside the general rules of werewolves. The idea of uncovering an ancient monster and that being the cause of the lycanthropy was inspired by Clive Barker's short story, Rawhead Rex, from *Books of Blood Volume 3*. It's a story that I thoroughly enjoyed, and the general set up was one that was easy to adapt into the deal-with-a-demon end of werewolf lore.

You'll note that the deal was less than voluntary in this instance, too. In the realms of horror, werewolves are commonly representative of a lack of control. Here, the demon also plays a part in this, taking control of the affected characters and pushing them along to match its own goals and needs. My thinking here was that it would play into one of the themes of the book: that certain things we do these days, often heavily influenced by others with a vested interest, makes us monsters, whether we want to be or not. At the same time, you can see by their actions after the change, which of the characters already had one foot in this dark side. After all, some people simply are cruel. You need only look on social media or the news to see that. Not all people are good, and many that are not, genuinely believe that they are.

That belief, whether justified or not, guides people's actions and strengthens their resolve.

Thematically, that point is touched on in a few ways in *The Beast of Loughby Island*. For example, Maggie Baker's declaration about civil disobedience eventually ceasing to be a theoretical last resort and becoming the only viable action left. This is a direct reference to the idea that it is the actions of others that change us and force us down other paths. Though she notes we usually have a choice in this, there comes times that that choice feels like it is taken away. Those outside forces—here, the demon— force people to react.

The idea of the curse being passed on by 'tooth and claw' ties into this. It is absolutely an intentional link to modern lore, designed to throw in something more familiar to readers relating to the concept of werewolves. It also represents the ways that people are affected, though. How many times have you felt something gnawing away at you or scratching in the back of your mind? How many times have those feelings made you think you need to do something about it? We've all been there. In reality, our eventual response takes time. It could be years of frustrations, or the eventual loss of hope, but we will react. We are simply built to have a breaking point, and there is always the risk that it will be breached.

As to the werewolf's weakness, I wanted to go back to the idea that you don't need silver. The purity aspect just didn't work for me here. I didn't want to head down the Christianity route, as this wasn't a story about that. That's why one of the creatures in the holy book Dougie found is based loosely on the description of an angel. Christianity is neither the hero nor the villain of the story because it's a story about humans. Plenty of humans use religion to justify bad behaviour, regardless of what the religion itself preaches. That is the only reason an angel-like being is mentioned at all in the book. This isn't a story where that path was chosen. Instead, we're looking at the repercussions of hate and anger. Think on this, though. People follow certain celebrities and prominent figures like religious idols, and take their word as gospel, no matter how ludicrous those words may be. Just because Christianity wasn't chosen in this story, doesn't mean the path of a zealot wasn't.

Regardless, you'll find no silver here. The werewolves are just tough. Really tough. To the point that the book leads up to a massive fight inspired by one of my favourite movies: *Dog Soldiers (2002)*. The cottage, set apart from the rest of the local populace, with a few survivors fighting for their lives, was lifted straight from that. Instead of military personnel facing off against a pack, we have two civilians and a cop fighting one monster. Using what they have to hand and their own skills to combat the threat is still the premise of the action. It's basically Spoon's kitchen brawl, but with more humans involved to make up for their lack of military training.

What that means is the rules of lycanthropy in The Beast of Loughby Island can be condensed down to:

The werewolf curse is obtained through summoning a specific entity that feeds on hate.

The curse is passed on by being bitten or scratched by a werewolf.

The shift occurs regardless of phase of the moon.

The werewolf is vulnerable to the same things as most humans, but is far tougher.

One thing I haven't touched on here is breaking the curse. You'll find in most popular media that there is no cure other than death. In fact, as even those who voluntarily became werewolves in older stories did so to cause suffering, they often ended up dead too. In cases involving a magical garment, you could simply stop wearing the item of clothing, I suppose. The devil isn't likely to just give you your soul back when you're bored of howling at the moon though, so bar God stepping in like he did in the second part of Johann Wolfgang von Goethe's tragedy, Faust, you were probably stuck in deal-making cases.

The nature of the curse is different in *The Beast of Loughby*

Island, though. Look at it as an extreme example of an agitator. When the cause being promoted has run its course, the one in control works to squeeze what little mileage is left out of it. Once it outlives its usefulness, the agitator moves on to another. Here, that means that the target of a person's genuine anger is eliminated, and so the demon then pushes them to stand against others, twisting their viewpoint to do so. Finally, Dougie Walters died, and the demon moved to Laura Atkins.

In some ways, the 'curse' remaining with one person at a time means it's more like a possession. That opened up an opportunity here for a cure, or an exorcism of sorts. Yes, the curse itself lived on through death, as the division it represents was still be present. Once the heroes physically cast out the demon, the cycle stopped.

Something to note: those that had changed in any way, remained physically changed. Dougie turned on those who cared about him. When he died, only a few recognisable scraps of what made him who he was remained. Laura was hateful to begin with, and the escalation of her usual behaviours left her more visibly monstrous on the outside.

Of the three survivors, Jennifer Gill was the outlier. She acknowledged the issues within the police force and showed her frustrations with this. She was also the only one to openly state that she hated the Atkins family. Consider then that when the heroes fought fire with fire, for Tom and Selwyn, that didn't feel like a choice. They were in a position where they were simply fighting for their lives. It was Jenn that directed them away from the town and encouraged them to fight. As she states at the end of the story, the good guys won and that mattered more than what had to be done to reach that outcome.

What that means is Jenn had already reached breaking point. She had accepted that confrontation was the only option left and willingly took part in that, dragging others along with her. As Maggie said, we all make choices, and there will always be consequences. This is why Jenn was also cursed. And while Tom and Selwyn successfully cast the demon out and brought an end to the cycle of hatred, Jenn was left with a physical reminder of the monster she had become to win the battle.

CREATING A MONSTER

When it came to designing the werewolf, I had a couple of things in mind. The first was that I'd noticed a piece of stock art that had been reused on several movie posters and DVD covers. Most importantly, it was always in cases where the werewolf in the movie did not look anything like the one in the picture. If you're curious, the films were *Among the Shadows*, *A Werewolf In England*, and *Carnivore: Werewolf of London*. In a tongue-in-cheek way, I wanted to pay tribute to that by taking some inspiration from the art.

It should also be noted that there has been an interesting evolution in the way werewolves have looked over the years. Back in the oldest movies, dogs were used, representing the person turning into an actual wolf. Then, we moved onto the wolfmen created by the legendary Jack Pierce, whose work on *Werewolf of London (1935)* brought us the first bipedal werewolf in cinema history. Eventually, we reached the vision that most of us think of when we hear the word werewolf: The bidepdal walking, but still more animal-leaning monsters, such as those in the Underworld series.

We have gone back and forth a little, of course. Rick Baker created what is, in my opinion, the greatest transformation scene of all time for *American Werewolf in London*, and that involved a quadrupedal wolf monster. You often see shifters having an animal form in Urban Fantasy too. The excellently fun Wolf Manor (2023) features something more akin to a modern wolfman design. But most people will still picture the hybrid when they hear the word werewolf. Whether that be the beautifully designed cover art on the limited-edition hardbacks of the previously mentioned High Moor Trilogy by Graeme

Reynolds, or the bulky masks and CG muzzles of many a lower budget production.

There is a surprising amount of variety to werewolf designs. So, this is where some of my personal tastes come into play. While I do love a big, hairy beast, I have more recently found myself to be really fond of the more sparsely furred werewolves you sometimes see. There have been some good examples of this. *13 Hrs (2010)* has a very nice design along those lines. Going back further, Ginger Snaps also has this, though I will admit to preferring the footage of the beast from the behind-the-scenes clips than how it looked in the final cut.

What I wanted to come up with was something that felt very natural. Like, if someone was to actually shapeshift, what would that look like? The stretched skin over the expanding bones and cartilage, and the way the foot elongates were an important part of that. I didn't want to get rid of the fur entirely, so made it sparse rather than prominent. No, I'm not saying that someone physically changing shape can look more natural than the sudden growth of excess body hair. There is a reason for this stylistic choice.

My intent was to create a feeling of unease by not quite being what you'd expect. The lack of a tail is there for the same reason. This look allows you to focus more on the body warping, because it's at the forefront of the design. I wanted it to be something you could picture, acknowledge as a monster, but still realise that it was in some way human. Going back to the themes of the story, even if you view someone as being a monster, no matter how justified that view may be, they are still human, after all.

THE IMPORTANCE OF THE SETTING

Equally as important here is the setting. Loughby Island is a fictional tidal island off the coast of Kent. I used this general location because I live in Kent, and have been enjoying putting out some stories based in my little corner of the world. The island itself came about because I was researching another monster that I want to write about: the Dobhar-chú.

Sometimes called the King Otter or Water Hound, the Dobhar-chú is a creature in Irish folklore that was spotted on Omey Island, which is a tidal island near County Galway. The concept of being cut off from the mainland by nature itself is one that lends itself to facing down a monster. You can't escape. You're stuck on the same landmass as it, and it's not a big area to run and hide in.

That Loughby Island is portrayed as being relatively idyllic for those that choose to live there makes the appearance of a werewolf all the more jarring for the characters. This was their little haven—a safe space if you prefer—and it is suddenly shattered by this violent, bloodthirsty beast of hate. Of course, it was never entirely a safe space. We learn quite quickly that the Atkins family are regular visitors, and their presence is one that the majority of residents view as disruptive. But that is something residents can ignore, as perfection is an unrealistic goal. The problem is, when things escalate, the sense of safety is shattered. Then, part of what makes the island so ideal for them—the natural cut-off from the mainland—becomes a major flaw.

This was designed to show that happiness can be shattered. Safety can turn to danger. And, cutting yourself off from the issues you're facing is only a temporary fix. We all need respite, and we all need to take care of ourselves. Until the demon is cast out, though, it can still find us, even on the most isolated yet welcoming of islands.

A FINAL WORD

This may not be the sort of werewolf story you're used to, or that you expected. You may even be wondering why I chose to write this particular tale. I'm going to be very honest here:

I wrote this book because I am pissed off.

The UK feels like a powder keg with a lit fuse slowly burning away. There's more division than at any other time of my life. The worst part is, it's all happening right in front of us. It's always the same prominent figures pushing the stuff that drives the wedges in. Extreme reactions are rapidly becoming the norm.

My books have always touched on things I view as important. The Cassie Tam Files warned that good people, no matter how stubborn and laser-focussed on doing the right thing they may be, can still wind up aiding the very people they're standing against. *Ailuros* spoke of identity, and the dangers of letting someone have too much influence over what we think and feel. Both contain anti-authoritarian sentiment. With *The Beast of Loughby Island,* that focus shifts to the effects of what I view as a rise in authoritarianism and normalisation of extreme views that is growing around us every day.

I see hate consuming people. I see good people who are doing nothing but living their lives being targeted and hurt. I see those of us trying to find ways to fix this picking the wrong fucking battles. It is a scary time to be alive.

I am well aware that this book will be divisive. I forewent some of my usual subtlety to make my point loud and clear here, because I felt that it was needed. But, if there was any doubt:

I am not calling for violence. I am saying hate is a monster that is devouring and infecting us all. I am saying that we need to fight the right battles. I am saying we need to be prepared for how messy this whole thing is going to get.

Most importantly, I am saying the good guys will win.

Stay strong. Resist hate. Fight on.

Matt Doyle

About the Author

MATT DOYLE is a pansexual/nonbinary author from the UK who primarily writes hybrid genre fiction with a sci-fi or horror grounding and diverse characters. In recent years, Matt's work has included the award-winning LGBTQ sci-fi mystery series, THE CASSIE TAM FILES, the experimental sci-fi horror novel, AILUROS, and several anthology appearances.

When not working on yet another story, Matt can usually be found taking on far too many other projects. This often includes voice acting, scare acting, costume building, pop culture blogging, and whatever else happens to pop up. You can find Matt in the following places:

https://mattdoylemedia.wordpress.com
https://www.facebook.com/MattDoyleMedia

www.ingramcontent.com/pod-product-compliance
Lightning Source LLC
Chambersburg PA
CBHW060504300726
48975CB00008B/2633